Whitehall Review

Rome's Recruits

Volume 8

Whitehall Review

Rome's Recruits
Volume 8

ISBN/EAN: 9783337300708

Printed in Europe, USA, Canada, Australia, Japan

Cover: Foto ©Andreas Hilbeck / pixelio.de

More available books at **www.hansebooks.com**

"Rome's Recruits:"

A List of

PROTESTANTS WHO HAVE BECOME CATHOLICS SINCE THE TRACTARIAN MOVEMENT.

Re-printed, with numerous additions and corrections, from

"The Whitehall Review"

Of September 28th, October 5th, 12th, and 19th, 1878.

PUBLISHED AT THE OFFICE OF "THE WHITEHALL REVIEW."
And Sold by James Parker & Co., 377, Strand, and at Oxford; and by Burns & Oates, Portman Street, W.

1878.

PREFACE.

—◆—

THE publication in four successive numbers of THE WHITEHALL REVIEW of the names of those Protestants who have become Catholics since the Tractarian movement, led to the almost general suggestion that Rome's Recruits should be permanently embodied in a pamphlet.

This has now been done.

The lists which appeared in THE WHITEHALL REVIEW have been carefully revised, corrected, and considerably augmented; and the result is the compilation of what must be regarded as the first List of Converts to Catholicism of a reliable nature.

While the idea of issuing such a statement of " Perversions " or " Conversions " was received with unanimous favour—for the silly letter addressed to the *Morning Post* by Sir Edward Sullivan can only be regarded as the wild effusion of an ultra-Protestant gone very wrong—great curiosity has been manifested as to the sources from whence we derived our information. The *modus operandi* was very simple. Possessed of a considerable nucleus, our hands were strengthened immediately after the appearance of the first list by

the co-operation of nearly all the converts themselves, who
hastened to beg the addition of their names to the muster-roll.

While the Roman Clergy have materially assisted us in the
compilation of the List of Recruits, it is worth noting that we
have had no help from the Cardinal Archbishop of Westminster,
nor from Monsignor Capel.   On the other hand, we have received
English additions to the List from all parts of the Continent,
and even from the United States.

The WHITEHALL List does not, of course, in any way repre-
sent the actual numbers of those who have gone over from the
Anglican to the Roman Communion.   But then it was no part of
our scheme to show how many have left us; all we essayed was
the publication of the names of the *élite*; and in this it is almost
impossible to say to what extent we have been successful.

THE EDITOR OF "THE WHITEHALL REVIEW."

November 8th, r878.

MR. GLADSTONE ON "ROME'S RECRUITS."

———◆———

Hawarden, Oct. 11, 1878.

DEAR SIR,

I thank you for sending me THE WHITEHALL REVIEW with the various lists of secessions to the Roman Church. I am glad they have been collected, and I am further glad to hear they are to be published in the form of a pamphlet. For good, according to some, or for evil, according to others, they form as a group an event of much interest and significance.

It would very *greatly* add to the value of the coming pamphlet if an approximate statement of dates could be made part of it. To give the year in each case would probably be very difficult; but would it be difficult to give decades? Say from 1820 or 1830. Even to divide yet more largely would still be useful; as thus:—

    1. Before 1840.
    2. 1840—60.
    3. Since 1860.

You will, I am sure, excuse this suggestion, and again accept my thanks.

I remain, your very faithful

W. E. GLADSTONE.

It would also be matter of interest to note:—

    1. The number of peers.
    2. Of members of titled families.
    3. Of clergy.
    4. Of Oxford men.
    5. Of ladies.

But perhaps you will leave all this to readers to extract for themselves.

ROME'S RECRUITS.

A

The Earl of Ashburnham.

John Bridge Aspinall, Q.C., Recorder of Liverpool.

Rev. W. H. Anderdon, M.A., Bennet Scholar of University College, Oxford; Vicar of St. Margaret's, Leicester. A Jesuit.

Rev. T. W. Allies, M.A., Fellow of Wadham College, Oxford; Chaplain to Bishop of London. Author of "The Church of England cleared from the charge of Schism;" "The See of St. Peter," &c., &c.

William E. Addis, M.A., Balliol College, Oxford. A priest of the oratory.

Bernard Addis. A Jesuit.

Rev. George Akers, M.A., Oriel College, Oxford. A priest.

H. A. Arden. A Dominican priest.

Frederic Antrobus, son of Baronet. Priest of the Oratory.

Commander Algar, R.N.

Rev. J. Algar, M.A., Fellow of University College, Oxford.

Thomas Arnold, M.A. (Oxford), youngest son of Dr. Arnold, of Rugby.

Arthur A'Beckett.

Chisholm Anstey, sometime M.P., and Attorney-General, Hong Kong.

Miss Aglionby.

Anne, wife of the 7th Duke of Argyll.

Rev. George Angus, B.A., Oxford; Curate of Prestbury. Priest.

Rev. Septimus Andrews, M.A., Student of Christ Church, Oxford; Vicar of Market Harbro'. A priest.

Lady A. Acheson.

Lady O. Acheson.

Lady Arundell, sister of the 1st Duke of Buckingham, and wife of the 10th Lord Arundell of Wardour.

The Duchess of Athole.

Rev. Joseph Atkinson, Priest of the Order of Charity.

Rev. E. W. Attwood, Curate of St. Leonard's, Shoreditch.

Walter Marsham Adams, B.A., Fellow of New College, Oxford.

Miss Agnew, daughter of Baronet, and author of "Geraldine."

The Lady Annaly.

Mrs. Weston Cracroft-Amcotts, wife of Colonel Cracroft-Amcotts, of Walcot Hall.

Henry V. Arkell. A priest.

— Arnold, University College, Oxford.

Miss Lloyd-Anstruther. A nun.

Mrs. Athy, Renville, Galway.

The Misses Adams.

Mrs. Anstice, widow of Rev. Joseph Anstice, of King's College, London.

Mrs. Robert Wigram Arkwright, of Normanton Turville Hall, Leicestershire.

Major-General Stewart Allan, Bengal Army.

Mr. and Mrs. Gilbert A'Beckett.

Mrs. Alleyne, widow of Rev. Joseph Alleyne, M.A., Oxford; two sons and a daughter.

Mrs. Adderley, sister-in-law of Lord Norton.

Henry Alexander, barrister-at-law.

Mrs. Arnott, widow of a clergyman.

Charles Francis Allnatt, Trinity College, Dublin; son of late Charles Blake Allnatt, of Shrewsbury, barrister-at-law.

Mrs. Ainsworth, North Wales. A nun.

Miss Arthur, Sister of Sir Frederic Arthur.

William Archer, Registrar-General, Victoria.

Hon. Mrs. Arbuthnot.

Miss Arbuthnot. A nun.

Mrs. Falconer Atlee.

Albert Atlee, and the Misses Atlee.

B

The Marquis of Bute.

Rev. Stuart Eyre Bathurst, M.A., Fellow of Merton College, Oxford; Rector of Kibworth Beauchamp, son of Sir James Bathurst, and grandson of Bishop of Norwich. A priest.

John Edward Bowden, author of the Memoirs of Father Faber. Oratorian.

Charles Henry Bowden. Oratorian.

Henry G. Sebastian Bowden, Scots Fusilier Guards. Oratorian.

John Bethell, brother of Lord Westbury. Augustus P. Bethell. A priest.

Rev. G. F. L. Bampfield, B.A., late scholar of Lincoln College, and First Class in Classics, Oxford. A priest.

Rev. Sir John Croker Barrow, Bart., M.A., Oxford.

Lady Barrow and Family.

Miss Barrow, sister of the Baronet.

Rev. Henry Bedford, M.A., St. Peter's College, Cambridge; Curate of Christ Church, Hoxton.

F. C. Burnand, author of "Happy Thoughts," &c., &c.

Henry Bellingham, M.A., S.C.L., Exeter College, Oxford; Barrister-at-Law, Private Chamberlain to Pope Leo. XIII.; eldest son of Sir Alan Bellingham, Bart, of Castle Bellingham, Co. Louth.

Mrs. Major Browne.

Rev. E. G. Kirwan Browne; Curate at Bawdsey, Norwich; nephew of Sir W. Nott, K.C.B.

Sir George Bowyer, Bart., M.P., D.C.L. (Oxford.)

Arthur Bovill, nephew of Lord Justice Bovill.

Rev. R. W. Brundritt, M.A., Christ College, Cambridge. A priest.

Rev. F. Bown, M.A., Curate of St. George's-in-the-East. A priest.

Edmund R. P. Bastard, M.A., Balliol College, Oxford, Double First Class; Kitley, Devon.

Rev. C. B. Bridges, M.A., Oriel College, Oxford.

Robert Braithwaite, B.A. (Oxford), barrister-at-law.

Isabella, wife of 8th Baron Beaumont, and daughter of 3rd Baron Kilmaine.

Henry, 9th Baron Beaumont.

W. H. Brown, B.A. (London).

Rev. W. H. Bliss, Magdalen College, Oxford, Rector of Hincksey.

Miss Tatton Browne.

Edward Badeley, M.A.

Sergeant Bellasis.

Rev. Professor Barff, M.A., Christ's College, Cambridge; Curate of Holy Trinity, Hull.

Rev. Robert Belaney, M.A., St. Catherine's College, Cambridge; Vicar of Arlington. A priest.

Rev. G. Burder, M.A., Magdalen Hall, Oxford; Curate at Ruardean. A Cistercian monk.

Rev. W. B. B; Brownlow, M.A., Trinity College, Cambridge; Curate at Torquay. A priest.

James Burns, Publisher.

Charles Alban Buckler, Architect.

Albert Buckler, now a Dominican monk.

Edmund Buckler, ditto.

Reginald Buckler, ditto.

Rev. Thomas Jones Burton, Curate at St. Paul's, Brompton.

Rev. Thomas Burton, M.A., Cambridge, Curate at St. James', Enfield. A priest.

J. G. Biggar, M.P.

Captain and Mrs. Boetler.

Rev. J. C. M. Bellew, M.A. (Oxford), the Elocutionist.

The Duchess of Buccleuch.

David Hunter Blair, son of Sir David Blair, Bart., M.A., Magdalen College, Oxford. A priest.

Miss Emily Bowles, author of several popular stories.

Richard Burchett, late Head Master of South Kensington Art Schools.

Rev. B. H. Birks, Curate at Arley. A priest.

Rev. H. Bittleston, M.A., St. John's College, Oxford, Curate at All Saints', Margaret Street. Priest of the Oratory.

Lewin Bowring, C.B., son of Sir John Bowring, Bengal C.S. Private Secretary to Lord Canning.

C. A. Bowring, Trinity College, Cambridge; son of Sir John. A Jesuit.

T. E. Bridgett, St. John's College, Cambridge. A priest.

Rev. William Hamilton Bodley, Curate of Tenison Chapel, Regent Street, Queen's College, Cambridge. A priest.

Henry Bacchus, Corpus Christi College, Cambridge.

Rev. H. Bayley, St. John's College, Cambridge. A priest.

Rev. W. Bell, St. John's College, Cambridge.

Rev. F. Balston, M.A., Christ Church, Oxford. A priest.

Rev. Frederick De Betham, Christ College, Cambridge. A Jesuit.

Rev. T. Bowdler, Curate of Tenison Chapel.

Rev. F. S. Bowles, M.A., Exeter College, Oxford. A priest.

W. H. Buckle, Controller of Customs.

Walter Buckle, Exeter College, Oxford. A priest.

Rev. Robert Butler, M.A., Brasenose College, Oxford; Warden of the House of Charity, Soho.

Rev. E. H. Ballard, M.A., Wadham College, Oxford. A priest.

George Frederic Ballard, Worcester College, Oxford. A priest.

Lieutenant Bastard, R.N.

Rev. Matthew Bridges, a contributor to the *Edinburgh Review*.

H. R. Bagshawe, Q.C., County Court Judge; son of Sir William Bagshawe, and father of the Bishop of Nottingham.

Mrs. Bagshawe, daughter of John Gunning, C.B.

The Earl of Buchan.

Mrs. Bridgman, Frogmore, Herefordshire.

Mrs. Boyce, Cheltenham.

Rev. Caithness Brodie, of Brodie; Curate of St. Stephen's, Kensington.

C. H. Bromby, St. Edmund Hall, Oxford, son of the Bishop of Tasmania.

Mrs. Barnes, of Gilling Castle, Yorkshire.

Mrs. and the Misses Bostock, Cheltenham.

E. G. Stanley Browne, St. Edmund Hall, Oxford.

Late Countess of Buchan.

Rev. J. W. Barlow.

W. S. Bosanquet.

Leicester Buckingham, Author.

Rev. George Whitefield Benjamin, D.D., Curate of the English Church at Rome.

Miss Bowring, daughter of Sir John Bowring. A nun at Hong Kong.

George Bentley, King's College, London.

Rev. William Maziere Brady, D.D.; Trinity College, Dublin; Chaplain to the Lord-Lieutenant. Chamberlain to the Pope.

Mrs. William Maziere Brady.

Captain Farmer Bailey.

Rev. G. R. Burrows, M.A., Queen's College, Oxford.

Miss Burnett.

Rev. Francis Bayly. Priest.

Rev. A. J. D. Bradley, B.A., Oxford; Curate of St. Martin's, Liverpool. Priest.

Mrs. Bengough and Miss Bengough.

Rev. Dr. Barrow, Principal of St. Edmund's Hall, Oxford. A Jesuit.

Lady Burke, daughter of the Right Hon. J. Calcraft.

Sir J. Bradstreet, Bart.

Rev. Evan Baillie, M.A., Trinity College, Oxford; Rector of Lawshall.

Mrs. Beckwith, wife of General Beckwith.

Rev. J. Harris Burton, Glenalmond Coll.; incumbent of St. John's, Selkirk.

Captain J. O. Burgoyne.

The Viscountess Bury.

Colonel and Mrs. Buckle.

James Britten, F.L.S., of the British Museum.

Clare, wife of Captain Joseph Boulderson, and daughter of J. C. M. Bellew, the elocutionist.

Evelyn Bellew, son of the elocutionist.

Harold Kyrle Bellew, ditto.

James Brown, LL.D.

Philip Burchett, author of well-known works on Geometry.

Arnold Baker, Exeter College, Oxford.

Mrs. Digby Boycott, senior.

Essex Digby Boycott.

Mrs. Essex Digby Boycott.

The Comtesse Geraldine Digby Boycott, Chanoinesse of the Royal Chapter of St. Anne, Munich.

Madame Mabel Digby Boycott. A nun.

Mrs. Blunt, of Crabbets, near Crawley, Sussex.

Rev. George Bampton. A Jesuit.

Francis Bacon, formerly lay-worker at St. Peter's, London Docks. A priest.

W. H. Bartlett. Dominican priest.

Francis G. Beresford, of the War Office.

Rev. H. G. J. Brasnell, Chaplain of Lincoln Gaol.

Rev. J. Carr Browne.

Rev. W. P. Burn, Incumbent near Rotherham.

Swinburne Berkeley.

Colonel Blair, Scots Fusilier Guards.

James Francis Wedderburn Bisshop, of Bramdean House, Hants.

Philip George Crosbie Bisshop.

R. C. A. Boyd, Corpus Christi College, Cambridge.

The Honourable Charles Bertie, late 47th Regiment, son of the Earl of Abingdon.

The Lady Elizabeth Bertie, daughter of the Earl.

The Lady Evelyn Bertie, ditto.

Mrs. Bacchus, daughter of late Professor Cumming, of Trinity College, Cambridge, and Rector of North Runcton.

Mr. and Mrs. Alexander Barclay.

Mrs. Richard Digby Beste, of Botleigh Grange, Hants.

Miss Bradley.

Captain F. Berthon, son of the Vicar of Romsey.

The Honourable George Bennett, Rifle Brigade.

J. Bentley, architect.

The late William Bond of St. Mawgan, Cornwall, with four sons (all priests) and four daughters (all nuns).

Alfred Bunn, librettist.

J. Baxter, Oxford, and Mrs. Baxter.

Miss Blunt, daughter of Consul at Smyrna.

Henry Charles Brandling.

Miss Beresford, niece of first Marquis of Waterford.

Miss Bathurst, granddaughter of Bishop Bathurst, of Norwich.

Miss Ballantine, daughter of Serjeant Ballantine.

Mrs. Hill Burton.

A. Blunden, son of Sir D. Blunden, Bart.

Benjamin J. Butland, Trinity College, Cambridge. A priest.

J. R. Beste.

Mrs. Brine, wife of Colonel Frederic Brine, R.E.

Mr. and Mrs. G. R. Buttemer.

Captain William Edward Buller, late 14th Light Dragoons.

Charles Bishop, solicitor ; Registrar of the Oxford County Court:

Mrs. Charles Bishop and Miss Bishop.

Clement Barraud. A Jesuit.

Miss Caroline Burke, daughter of Lady Burke.

Mrs. Bateman, wife of Dr. Bateman, of Folkestone.

Mrs. Beaumont, of Guildford.

Mrs. Raymond Barker, wife of nephew of Dr. Pusey, and two sons (one a Jesuit.)

J. G. H. Barnes, Wadham College, Oxford.

H. W. Brewer, architect.

William Brewer, Solicitor.

F. Orlando Bridgeman, of the Earl of Bradford's family.

Miss Busk.

Miss Bristow and Miss F. Bristow, daughters of Captain Bristow.

Miss Barnes.

George Beardmore.

Mrs. Blyth, wife of Rev. F. C. Blyth.

Mrs. Booth, Ashby Manor, Lincoln.

Mrs. Bayne, two sons and two daughters.

Miss E. Beresford, niece of the late Archbishop (Lord Decies) of Tuam.

The Honourable Mrs. Brown, granddaughter of the above Archbishop.

Mrs. Burrowes, great-granddaughter of the above Archbishop.

Mrs. Bishop (née O'Connor Morris).

Mrs. Andrew Brown, cousin of the late Bishop Forbes.

Miss N. G. Blunt.

Miss Blunt, daughter of Consul at Symrna.

Algernon Brown, son of Dr. Brown of Brighton.

John Biden. A Jesuit.

Captain Bathurst, R.N.

Captain Joseph Boulderson, late 68th Light Infantry.

Miss Diana Baring.

J. F. Boyd.

Mrs. Bliss, widow of Rev. William Bliss.

The late Sir Arthur Blennerhassett, Bart.

Madame Belloc (née Bessie Rayner Parkes), a Unitarian, a descendant of Dr. Priestley, and a well-known writer.

Joseph M. Browne, grandson of Captain Browne, R.N., of Sligo.

Mrs. Boynton, wife of Captain George Boynton, and aunt of Sir Henry Boynton, Bart.

John Bradney, of Bayford Lodge, son of clergyman.

Mrs. Bowyer, sister-in-law of Sir George Bowyer, Bart.

Mrs. Baumgardt, widow of Major-General John G. Baumgardt, C.B.

G. Bridgett, Assistant Commissary-General.

C. J. Bridgett.

Mrs. Hamilton Bradford.

James Browne, of Browneville, co. Galway.

Valentine Browne, C.E.

Mrs. Bleckly, wife of a clergyman, and her children.

Mrs. William Bocock, of Kirtling, Newmarket.

Miss Brand, sister of Speaker of the House of Commons.

Captain Gerard Bolton.

Alan H. Brodrick.

De la Barre, Bodenham, Herefordshire.

Henry Sherston Baker, M.A., Exeter College, Oxford.

Mrs. Brown, wife of Captain David Brown, 14th Light Dragoons.

Henry and Frederic Brown, of the East India Company's Service.

A. Gordon Breton, solicitor.

Mrs. Boyce, wife of Rev. W. Boyce, of Cheltenham College.

Captain Bernard, R.A., son of Rev. S. E. Bernard.

Mrs. J. M. Bellew, widow of the elocutionist.

Lady Caroline Barham, sister of the Earl of Thanet.

Madame Gaggiolti Barham, daughter of Lady Caroline Barham.

H. S. Butterfield, son of Rev. H. Butterfield, rector of Fulmer, Bucks.

Mrs. Blythe, wife of Captain Blythe.

Captain Francis Scawen Blunt, of the Rifle Brigade.

Miss Honoria Berwicke. A Sister of Charity.

Mrs. Bowden, daughter of the late Sir John Swinburne, Bart.

The late Miss Bowden. A nun.

Miss Emily Bowden.

The late Captain Henry Bowden, of the Guards. Founder of the Catholic Church at Chislehurst.

The late Mrs. Henry Bowden, née Burgoyne.

Miss Sarah Brigstocke.

C

The Countess Dowager of Clare.

Lord Courtenay.

Rev. Henry James Coleridge, M.A., Fellow of Oriel College, Oxford ; Scholar of Trinity, First Class in Classics, and brother of Lord Coleridge. A Jesuit.

Miss Coleridge.

Rev. G. L. Crawley, M.A., Christ Church, Oxford ; Curate of St. Saviour's, Leeds. A priest.

Frederick Capes, Proctor.

W. S. Coward, Trinity Hall, Cambridge, H.M. Inspector of Schools.

A. J. Christie, M.A., Fellow of Oriel College Oxford, First Class in Classics and Second in Mathematice. A Jesuit

Rev. Edward Caswall, M.A., Brasenose College, Oxford ; Curate at Stratford-under-the-Castle. A priest of the Oratory.

Rev. Verney Cave-Browne-Cave, son of Sir J. R. Cave-Browne-Cave, Bart. A priest.

Arthur B. Cumberlege, Trinity College, Cambridge. A priest.

Lady Chatterton, Authoress.

Rev. John Somers Cocks, Rector of Sheviock, Exeter.

Rev. Danvers Clarke, M.A., Exeter College, Oxford ; incumbent in Sussex and Rural Dean.

Richard Clarke, M.A., Fellow of St. John's College, Oxford. A Jesuit.

Rev. R. A. Coffin, Christ Church, Oxford, Rector of St. Mary Magdalen's, Oxford. A priest.

Rev. A. E. Coffin, Magdalen College, Oxford.

Rev. H. Coombes, Curate of St. Saviour's, Leeds.

William Chatto, M.A., Emanuel College, Cambridge. Built Catholic Church at St. Mary Church, Torquay.

Rev. C. Cholmondeley, Balliol College, Oxford. Priest and canon.

Rev. G. F. Case, M.A., Brasenose College, Oxford, Curate of All Saints', Margaret-street. Priest and Canon.

Rev. H. G. Coope, M.A., Christ Church, Oxford ; curate at Bucknell.

J. J. Calman, B.A., Worcester College, Oxford.

Mrs. Ross Church (Florence Marryat).

Miss Cusack, niece of Sir Ralph Cusack, known in Catholic literature as "the Nun of Kenmare."

Rev. C. W. Cavendish, M.A., Trinity College, Oxford ; rector of Casterton.

The late Mrs. Charles Cavendish.

Arthur V. L. Coombs, M.A., Oriel College, Oxford ; Captain Dorset Militia. Private Chamberlain to the late and to the present Pope.

Dr. Copeland, of Cheltenham.

Mrs. Copeland, née Bacchus.

J. A. Cook, Barrister-at-Law.

J. A. Charles. A priest.

Mrs. Clark, wife of Prebendary Clark, of Taunton.

Mrs. Codd, wife of Rev. E. T. Codd, Vicar of Bishop's Tachbrook, Warwickshire.

Mrs. Cholmeley, Brandsby Hall, Yorkshire.

Rev. John Coventry, M.A., Magdalen Hall, Oxford ; Rector of Tywardreath ; grandson of Earl of Coventry.

Alphonsus Coventry. A Servite priest.

Miss Cook, St. James's-square, Notting Hill.

Colonel Clifton, of Lytham, Lancashire.

Miss Clifton, daughter of Capt. and Lady Bertha Clifton.

Miss Cotton, daughter of the Provost of Worcester College, Oxford, and niece of Dr. Pusey.

Colonel Colthurst, brother of late Sir G. Colthurst, of Blarney, Co. Cork.

Joseph Clark, M.A., Magdalen College' Oxford. A Passionist priest.

Robert Colthurst.

J. Coleman, Worcester College, Oxford.

— Chandler, All Souls' College, Oxford.

Rev. C. Cox, B.A., Exeter College, Oxford.

The late Earl of Castlestuart.

Sir Gilbert E. Campbell, Bart.

Rev. Robert Campbell, M.A., Cambridge ; chaplain to Bishop of Aberdeen, and canon of Perth Cathedral.

R. D. B. Cunninghame, J.P., Hensol.

C. E. H. Edmonstoune-Cranstoun, J.P., Corehouse.

A. J. Cliffe, D.L., Bellevue, Wexford.

Captain Cliffe.

Captain Warner W. Carden.

Rev. Dr. J. T. Collett (Baptist).

Th. K. Chambers, M.A., M.D., Christ Church, Oxford.

Rev. F. C. A. Clifford, M.A., Cambridge ; Curate of Elveden, Suffolk.

Rev. Th. Lloyd Coghlan, sen., B.A., Trinity College, Dublin ; Rector of Mourne Abbey, Cork. A priest.

The late Mrs. T. L. Coghlan.

Rev. Th. L. Coghlan, jun., Curate at Stonehouse ; now Army Chaplain.

Rev. John Collins, M.A., Oxford ; Curat at Birkenhead.

Mrs. Hy. Clayton, of Ingatestone.

The Lady Chichester.

Captain Chichester, Dragoon Guards.

Miss Chambers, formerly Mother Eldress of the Devonport Sisters, under the direction of Miss Sellon

Mrs. Coxon, wife of M. A. Coxon, Bombay C. S., and daughter of Sir George Anderson, Governor of Ceylon.

Mrs. Attwell Coxon, of Hong Kong.

Major Archibald Chisholm.

Mrs. Caroline Chisholm (wife of the Major), "The Emigrant's Friend."

Rev. Dr. T. A. Crowther. Priest.

Mrs. Moreton-Craigie of Moreton Hall, Cheshire.

Miss Cope, daughter of Rev. Sir W. Cope, Bart.

Rev. H. Collins, curate at St. George's-in-the-East. Priest.

William Collis. Priest and Canon.

Robert Clarke, M.R.C.S. A priest.

J. Cookesley, M.D.
The Honourable Mrs. Woodhouse Currie, daughter of Lord Lyveden.
Rev. A. D. R. Campbell, Curate of Ashley, Newmarket.
Rev. H. W. Challis, M.A.; scholar of Merton College, Oxford.
Mrs. Cannon, wife of General Cannon, of Folkestone, and the Misses Cannon.
Arthur Charles Croker, formerly an officer of the 77th Regiment, and son of the late Colonel Croker of the 18th Hussars.
Mrs. and Miss Comyn, of Plymouth.
Charles Comberbach. Priest.
Miss Ellen Cottam.
W. A. Osborne Christmas, nephew of W. Christmas, formerly M.P. and D.L. of Whitfield, Waterford.
Mrs. and Miss G. Veronica Christmas.
The Lady Katherine Coke, daughter of the Earl of Wilton.
Miss Crosse.
The Lady Codrington.
Henry Clutton, architect.
Anthony Cope, son of Rev. Sir W. Cope, Bart.
Mrs. Anthony Cope.
Mrs. Bertram Currie.
Captain Cox.
Miss Claxton, now Marchesadi Salvo.
Augustus Craven, husband of the author of "Le Récit d'une Sœur."
Mrs. John Coventry, wife of clergyman.
Henry Ferrers Croxon.
Compton Croxton.
Constance Croxton.
Mrs. Campbell, wife of the member for North Staffordshire.
Mrs. Cooper, wife of Colonel Morse Cooper.
John Cooper.
H. Stonehewer Cooper.
Charles Cholmondeley, a Cheshire squire, brother of Mr. Cholmondeley, of Condover Park, Salop, and nephew of Bishop Heber. A priest.
Mrs. John Christie, of Stanley Crescent, Notting Hill.
C. H. Clarke, M.D.
Dr. Counsellor.
Francis Macnamara Calcutt, formerly M.P. for County Clare.
Arthur L. Chattaway. A priest.
W. W. Cook. A priest.
George E. Clerk, brother of Sir Douglas Clerk, Bart., of Penicuik.
Mrs. and Miss Lane Clarke, Guernsey.
Lady Adelaide Cathcart.
Lady Katherine Elizabeth Cochrane, daughter of the 10th Earl of Dundonald.
Mrs. Henry Caulfield.
Miss Carnsew, sister-in-law of Dean Cowie, of Manchester.
Mrs. Charles Cliffe.

Miss Churchill, daughter of Major-General Churchill.
Alderman Chambers, ex-Mayor of Margate.
Miss Chandless, daughter of the Q C. A nun.
Andrew Currie, sculptor.
Mr. Carew, of the War Office.
Thompson Cooper, journalist and author.
Miss Laura Chesshyre, daughter of a clergyman.
Miss Margaret Wyatt Cobb.
Mr. and Mrs. William Codrington, Wroughton House, Swindon.
The Honourable Miss Crewe, sister of Lord Crewe.
Mrs. Coates, of Reigate.
H. Considine, D.L., Derk.
Mrs. Clutterbuck, sister of Sir John Croker Barrow, Bart.
Mrs. Crowe, wife of Captain Crowe, of Folkestone.
The Honourable Mrs. Colonel Clifford.
Mrs. Moss Cooper, sister of Mr. Walter, M.P., of *The Times*.
Miss Courtenay, sister of the Bishop of Jamaica.
James Carter, Priest and Chamberlain to the late Pope.
Miss Clifford, of Carne, co. Cavan.
Miss Wilmot Chetwode, daughter of Edmund and Lady Janet Wilmot Chetwode, of Woodbrook, Queen's County.
Miss Janet Wilmot Chetwode.
Miss Carrington, daughter of a clergyman.
Henry Cowell. A Jesuit.
Archibald D. L. Campbell, nephew of D. Campbell, of Lochnell.
Donald C. V. Campbell, son of James Archibald Campbell, of Inverawe. A Jesuit.
Joseph Corbett. A priest.
Mrs. Chirol, wife of Rev. A. Chirol.
Mrs. Clavering, of Callaly.
Captain and Mrs. Collard, of Walthamstow.
Mrs. Connolly. A nun.
Baronne de Corson, relative of Cardinal Manning.
Miss Christian, sister of Judge Christian.
Duchess de Sforza Cesarini, née Caroline Shirley.
Edwin Chabot, Churchwarden of St. James', Hatcham.
Captain Cuffe, of Connaught.

D

The Earl of Denbigh.
Rev. Nicholas Darnell, M.A., Fellow of New College, Oxford; son of the Rector of Stanhope. A priest.

The Countess D'Albanie, widow of the late Count D'Albanie.

Lady Alice, wife of Count Stuart d'Albanie, and daughter of 17th Earl of Erroll.

Edward Heneage Dering, of the Coldstream Guards, author of "Sherborne" and other novels.

J. B. Dalgairns, M.A., Exeter College, Oxford. An eminent writer in the *Contemporary Review*, and elsewhere. A priest of the Oratory.

Lord Archibald Douglas, son of 7th Marquis of Queensberry. A priest.

Lady Gertrude Douglas.

Dr. Duke, of Hastings.

Dr. Duke, of St. Leonard's.

Captain Dashwood, of Torquay.

Sir Charles Douglas, author of "Long Resistance and ultimate Conversion."

Lady Douglas.

Sir Vere de Vere, Bart.

The Lady De Vere.

Aubrey de Vere, the poet.

Stephen de Vere, some time M.P. for Limerick.

The late Lady de Trafford.

C. Devas, M.A., Balliol College, Oxford.

Ambrose Phillipps de Lisle, of Garendon Park and Grace Dieu Manor, Leicestershire.

Kenelm H. Digby, Trinity College, Cambridge, author of "The Broadstone of Honour," &c.

Rev. T. Dykes, M.A., Clare College, Cambridge, Curate at Hull. A Jesuit.

Captain Dewell, Jesuit Lay Brother.

Rev. Edward B. Deane, D.C.L., Fellow of All Souls' College, Oxford; Rector of Lewknor.

Mrs. E. Deane.

Rev. T. D. Dove, A M., Emmanuel College, Cambridge; curate of St. Mary Magdalen's, Munster-square.

J. H. Dale, Trinity College, Camb., Curate of Frome Selwood. A priest.

Rev. W. Dodsworth, B.D., Camb., Vicar of Christ Church, St. Pancras.

Rev. J. Douglas, B.A., Christ Church, Oxford; curate of Emscote. A priest.

H. Denny, St. John's College, Oxford.

Sir Charles and Lady d'Albiac.

Joseph Davenport, B.A., Jesus College, Cambridge.

R. De Barry, Weston Hall, Warwickshire.

The late Earl of Dunraven.

The Honourable Lady Duncan.

Miss Duncan, daughter of the Hon. Lady Duncan.

Sir Compton Domvile, Bart.

Rev. Alfred J. Dayman, B.A., Exeter College, Oxford; Curate of Wasperton.

Miss D'Eyncourt.

Mrs. D. E. Dewar.

Rev. D. Erskine Dewar, Fellow of New College, Oxford; rector of Friestho pe.

Wm. Douglas Dick, of Tullymet.

Richard Hay Drummond, of Hawthornden, son of late Sir Hay Drummond, Bart., and desendant of the poet.

Madame D'Arras, daughter of late Sir E. H. Lechmere, Bart.

Rev. Hubert De Burgh, Curate at Lawshall. A priest.

George Dover, M.A., Exeter College Oxford. A Jesuit.

— Dawe, of St. Mary Hall, Oxford. A priest.

Rev. J. P. Durell, University College, Oxford; now Tutor, Catholic University College, Kensington.

The Honourable Mrs. Robert Daly.

Mrs. Archibald Dunn.

The Honourable Mrs. Captain J. B. Dormer.

Mrs. Miles Dormer.

Thomas Drinkwater. A priest.

Captain Dugmore, 64th Regt.

The Honourable Mrs. Dugmore, daughter of Lord Brougham.

Rev. Alexander Donaldson, curate at Farmborough.

Mrs. George Dunn, of Harley-street.

J. C. Dunn, B.A., New College, Oxford.

Mr. and Mrs. C. D. Dyatt.

Rev. Joshua Dixon, Brasenose College, Oxford. A missionary priest in Texas.

J. W. W. Drew, M.A., St. Alban's Hall, Oxford. A priest.

Rev. William V. Dawson, M.A., Oxford. Incumbent in Diocese of Ripon.

C. E. B. Davis, B.A., London.

Mrs. De Burgh, wife of the Vicar of West Drayton.

Rev. C. H. Dixon, Curate at Fewston.

Mary, wife of Marmaduke Dolman, Barrister-at-law, and daughter of Major Waud, late of Chester Court and Manston Hall, Yorks.

W. E. Dobson, J.P., The Park, Nottingham.

Miss Du Boulay, of Torquay. A nun.

Mrs. Duff.

The Honourable Mrs. Davison, widow of General Davison, and daughter of Lord Graves.

Rev. Joseph Darlington, Brasenose College, Oxford.

Archibald Donaldson, nephew of Professor Donaldson.

Charles Dawson, Pembroke College, Oxford.

The Misses Dashwood, daughters of Admiral Dashwood.

Rev. John Tindal Durell, St. Peter's College, Cambridge.

Mr. and Mrs. C. F. Dashwood, of St. Michael's Torre, Devon.

Mrs. Dunlop, wife of Admiral Dunlop.

Captain Dunlop, son of Admiral Dunlop, C.B.

Mrs. Darcy, wife of Colonel Darcy, late Governor of the Falkland Islands.

Mrs. Warren Darley.

Henry Warren Darley.

Mrs. Colonel Dorat.

Miss Drane, author of "Christian Schools and Scholars," and other works. A Dominican nun.

The Misses Dunsford.

Mrs. Dayman, wife of the Rector of Shillingstone.

The Hon. Mrs. De Moleyns, widow of the Hon. Colonel De Moleyns.

Mrs. De Gernon, of Athcarne Castle (née Braham), niece of Lady Waldegrave.

Rev. Edward B. Douglas. Priest and canon.

Madame De la Haye, sister of Dowager Lady Inchiquin.

Lady Elizabeth Douglas, daughter of the 2nd Earl Cathcart.

Mrs. Dawson, daughter of Admiral Sir Michael Seymour, and widow of Colonel Dawson, 90th Regiment.

Miss Dawson, Miss Lina Dawson, and Miss Effie Dawson, daughters of above.

Mrs. Dobson, wife of William E. Dobson, J.P.

H. Davey of the War Office.

The Honourable Mr. Dillon, late of the Home Office.

James Dees, J.P., Northumberland.

Captain and Mrs. Davidson, of Folkestone.

Mrs. Doughan, Orrell Park, Aintree.

Frederic Smith-Dodsworth, son of Sir Charles Smith-Dodsworth, Bart.

Mrs. Frederic Smith-Dodsworth.

Countess de Damas de Hautefort, née Young.

Captain W. N. Darnell, 84th Regiment.

Mrs. W. N. Darnell.

Mrs. Duke, sister of Dowager Duchess of Argyll.

Lady Elizabeth Douglas, sister of Marchioness of Queensberry.

Sister Drummond and Miss M. Drummond, son and daughter of Maurice and the Hon. Mrs. Drummond.

Miss Danvers, of Chiselhurst.

Miss Dixon, daughter of General Dixon. A nun.

E

The Lord Emly, some time Postmaster-General.

W. Martin Edmunds, Trinity College, Cambridge.

Rev. John Charles Earle, B.A., Oriel College, Oxford, Curate at Ongar; Author of Poems.

V. D. H. Carey Elwes, Billing Hall, Northamptonshire.

Rev. Edgar E. Estcourt, M.A., Exeter College, Oxford; curate at Cirencester. A priest and canon.

Rev. T. A. Eaglesim, M.A., Worcester College; Curate of St. Paul's, Oxford.

Henry A. Eliot, Merton College, Oxford.

Charles O. Eaton, M.A., Trinity College, Cambridge, D.L., Tolethorpe Hall, Stamford.

Mrs. Eaton.

Rev. George B. Erskine, M.A., Merton College, Oxford.

F. C. Ellis, Queen's College, Oxford.

J. Ellis, St. John's College, Oxford.

Captain Windsor Carey Elwes, Scots Guards.

Rev. W. Eye of St. George's Mission.

Rev. — Edwards, Curate of St. Matthias', Stoke Newington.

Richard Eaton, D L., Barrister-at-law.

Mrs. Richard Eaton.

Dr. Ewart, M.D.

Captain Ellerby, R.A.!

A. T. Wyatt-Edgell, Christ Church, Oxford.

The Honourable Mrs. Wyatt-Edgell, daughter and co-heiress of the Baroness Braye.

Miss Wyatt-Edgell.

Miss Caroline M. Edgar, authoress.

John Eustace, Quaker.

Miss Earle, daughter of an Essex vicar.

William Edgcome. A Jesuit.

Richard Edgcome. A priest.

Mrs. Eyre and Miss Caroline Eyre.

F

The late Viscountess Fielding.

Alexander G. Fullerton, some time Attaché at the French Embassy.

Lady Georgiana Fullerton, sister of the present Earl Granville.

George Lane Fox, jun., Christ Church, Oxford; Bramham, Yorkshire.

The late Mrs. George Lane Fox, daughter of General Slade.

Rev. Frederick W. Faber, Fellow of University College, Oxford; Rector of Elton; founder of the Brompton Oratory and a voluminous writer.

Rev. Ed. Bowles Knottesford Fortescue, M.A., Wadham College, Oxford; Dean of St. Ninian's, Perth, and brother-in-law of the Archbishop of Canterbury.

Hon. Mrs. Percy Fitzgerald, daughter of 10th Viscount Massereene and Ferrard.

Henry Foley, solicitor. A Jesuit Lay Brother.

Dr. Fincham, M.A., St. John's College, Oxford.

Rev. Henry Formby, M.A., Brasenose College, Oxford; Rector of Ruardean. A priest.

J. F. Flockhart, Jesus College, Camb.

Rev. Comte de la Felde, Vicar of Fortington, Chichester.

Field-Marshal Sir J. Foster Fitzgerald.

Lady Louisa Fitzgibbon, daughter of the late Earl of Clare.

Jas. Ogilvie Fairlee, B.A., Christ Church, Oxford; and his brother.

Gerald C. Purcell Fitzgerald, M.A., Trinity College, Cambridge.

Rev. Wm. Felgate, Trinity College, Cambridge.

Rev. Wm. Fothergill, Curate of St. Paul's, Knightsbridge.

Thos. Foster, LL.D., Trinity College, Cambridge.

Mrs. William Froude, sister-in-law of the historian.

Hurrell Froude, nephew of historian.

Edmund Froude, ditto.

Miss Froude, niece of historian.

Miss Fane, daughter of Prebendary Fane.

Rev. John Frederick Fagge, B.A., University College, Oxford; Vicar of Aston Cantlow; brother of the Baronet.

Mrs. Fagge.

Rev. P. Fletcher, B.A., Exeter College, Oxford; Curate of St. Bartholomew's, Brighton.

Rev. Alfred Fawkes, M.A., Balliol College, Oxford; ditto.

Miss Christina Forbes, of Invernan.

The Lady Featherstone.

William Farren, the actor.

Dr. Fowler and family, of Cheltenham.

Reginald Fowler, son of Dr. Fowler of Cheltenham. A priest.

Rev. T. Burnes Floyer, J.P. for County of Stafford.

Rev. C. J. P. Forster, Curate at Stoke Abbas; and Mrs. Forster.

Rev. W. G. Freeman, of Plymouth.

Mrs. W. G. Freeman.

Rev. G. Ford, Curate of St. Mary's, Soho.

George French Flowers, Musical Doctor, Oxford.

Henry Frye, late of Madras Army.

Miss Mary Dominica Ford, foundress of St. Margaret's Home.

The Lady Forster, wife of Sir Charles Forster, M.P., of Lysways Hall, Stafford.

Mrs. John Fottrell.

Mrs. Fuller, widow of Captain Fuller the sculptor.

F. J. F. Fegen, Barrister-at-law.

Colonel and Mrs. Flamstead.

Miss Fountaine, daughter of Andrew Fountaine, of Narford Hall, Norfolk.

Miss Foljambe.

The late James Firebrace, attorney.

Miss Geraldine Penrose Fitzgerald, sister of R. W. Penrose Fitzgerald of Corkbegg Castle, County Cork.

The late Samuel Firebrace, LL.D., Judge at Demerara; his three sons and two daughters.

Cottenham Farmer, M.D., and Mrs. Farmer.

Mrs. Ferrers.

W. F. Finlason, barrister-at-law.

Laurence C. Prideaux Fox, a Quaker. A priest.

Mr. and Mrs. Joseph Fothergill, Whickham Park, near Newcastle-on-Tyne.

Charles, Augustus, John, Valentine, and Louis, sons of the Hon. Gerald and Lady Louisa Fitzgibbon.

Miss Florence Fitzgibbon. A nun.

J. H. Flesher, B.A., Christ's College, Cambridge.

Miss Ellen France, built the Church at Leamington.

Mrs. Saville Foljambe.

Emma and Cecilia, daughters of Vice-Admiral Sir T. F. Freemantle, Bart.

Reginald Forbes, cousin of the late Bishop of Brechin.

Mrs. Miles Fletcher.

Mrs. Ferrers, of Baddesley Clinton.

The Lady Elizabeth Foote, daughter of 5th Marquis of Queensberry.

Mrs. J. A. Fox, youngest daughter of the late Count W. F. Wratislaw, of Rugby.

Mrs. Fortescue, granddaughter of Lady Caroline Barham.

William Foster, solicitor, Alnwick.

Dr. Farmer.

Richard FitzPatrick, brother of Lord Castletown.

Robert Fetherstone, J.P. for co. Limerick.

G

The Earl of Gainsborough.

The Countess of Gainsborough.

Ignatius Grant, St. John's College, Oxford. A Jesuit.

Rev. E. S. Grindle, M.A., "Presbyter Anglicanus," late Scholar of Queen's College, Oxford; curate of St. Paul's, Brighton.

Earl of Granard.

Colonel W. H. Graham.

Rev. C. B. Garside, M.A., Brasenose College, Oxford; Curate of All Saints', Margaret-street. A priest.

Nathaniel Goldsmid, M.A., Exeter College, Oxford.

Mrs. Nathaniel Goldsmid.

Mrs. Milner Gibson, wife of former M.P.

John Godard, celebrated in early photography.

Thomas Gaisford, J.P.

Lady Alice Gaisford.

Edward Dwyer Gray, M.P., Proprietor of "The Freeman's Journal."

Theodore Galton, M.A., Trinity College, Cambridge; Hadzor, Worcestershire.

Rev. John Melville Glenie, M.A., St. Mary's Hall, Oxford; Perpetual Curate of Mark. A Priest and canon.

F. J. Gordon, St. Peter's College, Cambridge.

Rev. J. Gordon, Curate of Christ Church, St. Pancras, London. A Priest of the Oratory.

Rev. R. Gordon, M.A., Oriel College, Oxford.

Miss Gladstone, sister of the Right Hon. W. E. Gladstone, M.P.

Philip Gordon. A Priest of the Oratory.

Rev. T. Goodwin, Chaplain of Christ Church, Oxford.

H. de G. Grissell, B.A., Brasenose College, Oxford. Chamberlain to the Pope.

Colonel Gerard, of Rocksoles, Scotland.

Rev. Harman Grisewood, B.A., Christ Church, Oxford; Daylesford House.

The Lady Grey, daughter of Admiral Sir Robert Spencer.

Rev. A. B. Gurdon, M.A., Cambridge. A priest.

J. Grainger, Chamberlain to the Pope.

Rev. Philip Gurdon, M.A., University College, Oxford; rector of Ossington.

The Hon. Ashley Carr Glyn, University College, Oxford.

Salmon Grouse, Queen's College, Oxford. Bengal C.S.

Rev. William Goldstone, St. Michael's, Wakefield.

Rev. T. H. Grantham, Curate of Slinfold, Sussex.

Mrs. T. H. Grantham, wife of ex-curate of Slinfold.

Rev. J. J. Greene, M.A., Curate of St. Bartholomew's, Brighton.

Mrs. Galton, wife of Rev. J. L. Galton, Rector of St. Sidwell's, Exeter.

Hugh Gladstone, cousin of the late Premier.

Mrs. Greatheed, of Prestbury, Cheltenham.

Rev. W. Rees Gawthorn.

Rev. Dr. Göltz, Christ College, Cambridge; Rector of Christ Church, Southwark.

James Grant, the novelist.

The late Countess of Granard.

The Lady Gray of Gray.

Miss Gordon, of Prince's Gate.

Miss A. M. Gordon, of Abergeldie.

Rev. F. Peel Garnett, M.A., Brasenose College; Curate of Trinity Church, Oxford. Priest of oratory.

Major F. W. Garnett, late 85th Regiment.

H. Percy Garnett, 32nd Regiment.

Mrs. Gruggen, wife of Vicar of Pocklington.

Samuel Grimshaw, Erwood Hall, Buxton.

Mrs. Graham, of Wimbourne.

Everard Green, F.S.A.

Mrs. Goodlake.

Colonel Pollock Gore.

Mrs. Douglas Cunningham Graham.

Miss E. Cunningham Graham.

Mrs. Garnett, daughter of Colonel F. H. Custance.

Arthur H. Galton, Clare College, Cambridge.

Le Marchant Gosselin, Christ Church, Oxford.

Robert H. Gosselin.

Mrs. Grisewood.

Mr. Gatty, son of Mrs. Alfred Gatty.

Major Gape, of St. Albans.

The Lady Guy, widow of Sir Philip Guy.

E. Garnett.

Mrs. Charles Martin Green, Newcastle-on-Tyne.

Miss Gream, daughter of the Rector of Rotherfield.

Miss Hilda Gream, daughter of Rev. Nevile Gream, Inspector of Schools.

Baker Gabb, lawyer, of Abergavenny.

Miss Galton, Glengariffe, Bournemouth.

G. R. Gordon, Ellon Castle, Aberdeenshire, grandson of Lord Aberdeen.

F. W. E. Gruggen, solicitor.

Mr. and Mrs. Malcolm Grant.

The Misses Grenfell.

I. Goddard, now Rector of St. Mary's, Chislehurst, and a monsignor.

Mrs. Gretton, of Swindon Hall, Gloucestershire.

Mr. and Mrs. George Gretton.

Thomas Grinfield, son of Rev. Thomas Grinfield.

Rev. Andrew Green, M.A., Trinity College, Cambridge; Curate of St. Paul's, Oxford.

Mrs. Andrew Green.

Mrs. Green, née Biddulph, co. Tipperary.

Mrs. Gavin, wife of Major Gavin, co. Limerick.

Mrs. Grace, of Gracefield, née Thistlethwaite.

Lawrence Gardiner. A Dominican priest.

Mrs. Gernon, Athcarne Castle, co. Meath, daughter of Major Braham.

A. W. Garrett, B.A., Balliol College, Oxford.

Mrs. Grant, wife of a clergyman.

Miss Grant, sister of Sir Alexander Grant, of Edinburgh University.

Powell Baker Gabb, son of Monmouthshire rector.

John and Charles Augustine Baker Gabb, of Abergavenny.

H

Rev. William J. M. Hutchison, S.C.L., Saint Mary Hall, Oxford ; Curate of St. Endellion, Cornwall. Private Chamberlain to Pope Leo XIII.

Mrs. W. J. M. Hutchison.

The Lady Herbert of Lea, mother of Lord Pembroke and of Lady Lonsdale.

Lady Mary Herbert, now Baroness Mary Von Hügel.

S. Taprell Holland.

William Antony Hutchison, Trinity College, Cambridge. A priest.

Rev William C. Hutchinson.

Rev. Robert Stephen Hawker, Vicar of Morwenstowe.

Rev. Thomas Henry. A Priest.

Rev. W. M. Hunnybun, M.A., Caius College, Cambridge ; vicar of Bickernoller.

Mrs. W. M. Hunnybun.

Rev. Douglas Hope, M.A., Christ Church, Oxford ; curate of St. Agnes, Kensington.

Rev. A. J. Hanmer, of Tiverton.

Captain Washington Hibbert, of Billing Hall.

Rev. Thomas Norton Harper, B.A., Queen's College, Oxford ; Incumbent of St. Peter's, Buckingham Palace Gate. A Jesuit.

Rev. W. Harper, M.A., Pembroke College, Oxford.

Miss Harris, author of " From Oxford to Rome."

The Duchess of Hamilton.

Rev. Frederick Hathaway, M.A., Fellow of Worcester College ; Curate of St. Mary Magdalen's, Oxford. A Jesuit.

S.J. Hughes, eldest son of Thomas Hughes, of Reigate.

Rev Russell Howell, M.A., Christ Church, Oxford ; Vicar of St. Veep, Cornwall.

Mrs. Russell Howell.

Rev. C. Hamilton, Exeter.

Edward Hood, Solicitor. A Jesuit.

The late Lord Huntingtower.

Rev. William Humphrey, Vicar of St. Mary Magdalen's, Dundee, and Chaplain to Bishop of Brechin. A Jesuit Priest.

Sylvester Hunter, Trinity College, Cambridge ; Barrister-at-law ; son of the late Joseph Hunter of the Public Record Office. A Jesuit Priest.

Rev. John Headlam, M.A., Pembroke College, Cambridge.

Edward Owen Hornby, M.A., St. John's College, Cambridge.

E. J. Hutchins, Trinity College, Cambridge. Some time M.P.

Rev. John Houghton, Trinity College, Cambridge.

William Perceval Heathcote, eldest son of the Right Hon. Sir Wm. Heathcote, Bart., of Hursley.

Mrs. Heathcote, widow of late Rev. W. B. Heathcote, Fellow of New College, Oxford, and Precentor of Salisbury.

Rev. J. Henn, Curate of St. James', Bristol.

Rev. Samuel Harper, M.A., Trinity College, Cambridge ; Rector of St. Ninian's, Perth.

Lady Katherine Howard.

Lady Harris.

General J. Caradoc, 2nd Lord Howden, G.C.B.

Admiral Robert Hall, Secretary to the Admiralty.

Henry Edward Fox, last Lord Holland.

Rev. E. Horne, M.A., St. John's College, Cambridge ; Vicar of St. Lawrence, Southampton.

Mrs. Horne, two daughters. Both nuns.

The Hon. Mrs. Heneage.

James Harris. A Jesuit.

Captain W. Harrison, R.A.

Mrs. Houldsworth of Craigforth, Stirling.

Mrs. Craigie-Halkett, of Cramond, Midlothian.

Rev. John Higgins, B.A., St. John's College, Cambridge ; Curate of Taunton. A priest.

Rev. C. E. Hodson, M.A., Trinity Hall, Cambridge ; Chaplain to the Arctic Expedition.

Rev. Evan Haynes Hunter, Trinity College, Cambridge. A priest.

Rev. Arthur W. Hutton, M.A., Exeter College, Oxford, Rector of Spridlington, Lincolnshire. An oratorian.

Daniel Haigh. A priest ; built church at Erdington.

The Lady Heywood, wife of Sir Percival Heywood, Bart.

The Hon. Mrs. Henniker.

Rev. William Hutcheson, Rector of Ubley.

The late Major John F. Haliburton.

Wyndham H. Nelson Hoste, B.A., Christ Church, Oxford, brother of the late Rear-Admiral and Baronet. Barrister-at-Law.

Rev. H. J. Hardy, M.A., Oxford.

Rev. W. J. Hardy.

E. B. Harding, Exeter College, Oxford, a nephew of Dr. Pusey ; now organist at Birmingham Oratory.

The Lady Holland.

Miss M. Hamilton, niece of Lord Dillon.

Miss Head, daughter of Sir Edmund Head, Governor-General of Canada.

The late Matthew Higgins, the " Jacob Omnium " of the *Times*.

Colonel Hibbert, Royal Canadian Rifles.

William Henry Hart, F.S.A., solicitor.

J. R. Herbert, Royal Academician.

Gerard R. Hopkins, B.A., Balliol College, Oxford. A Jesuit.

N. H. Higginson, Exeter College, Oxford. Annie Emra Holmes, Canoness of St. Augustine, Bruges.

Mary Holmes, author of "Hints on Music."

Thomas Helmore, son of Rev. T. Helmore, Precentor of H.M. Chapel Royal.

Mrs. Hare, sister-in-law of Archdeacon Hare.

Rev. George Harper, brother of Protestant Australian Bishop. A Jesuit.

Francis Buchanan Hoare.

— Harvey, Hertford College, Oxford.

Herbert Harrison, Captain of Westminster School. Oratorian novice.

Rev. S. Hill, curate near Exeter.

Rev. G. H. Hill, Rector of Saltford.

Rev. J. Hammond, of St. George's Mission.

Miss Hannah Hedley. A nun.

Miss Fanny Hedley.

Miss Harding, of St. Mary Church, Torquay.

Colonel Holt.

Miss Hanmer, sister of Lord Hanmer.

Charles Hallé, the pianist.

The Honourable Mrs. Herbert of Llanarth, daughter of Lord Llanover.

Miss Henry.

Davie Haye, of the Middle Temple.

Rev. — Hetling, M.A., Curate of St. Peter's, Plymouth.

Mrs. Hope, The Hermitage, Torquay.

Miss Margaret Hinson, daughter of the late Vicar of Horton.

Miss Flora Horn, daughter of Henry Horn, sometime Recorder of Hereford. A nun.

Richard H. Hawkes, of Bristol.

Mrs. Hamilton, wife of the late Captain J. F. C. Hamilton, R.N.

Miss Hamond, granddaughter of the late Archbishop (Lord Decies) of Tuam.

Henry Nunez Heysham, formerly of Alresford.

Miss Hutchinson, daughter of the Rector of Checkley.

Miss Hayne, daughter of a clergyman.

Dr. and Mrs. Harris

Assistant-Commissary Hunter, Dublin.

Lewis Hunt, M.D.

The late Honourable Mrs. Hewett, wife of Lord Lifford's eldest son.

Mr. and Mrs. Arthur Hornby, of Fareham, Hants.

Lady Frances Howard, daughter of 4th Earl of Wicklow.

Lady Anne Jane Howard, daughter of 4th Earl of Wicklow.

Miss Hodgson, one of the Anglican nuns who accompanied the "Cowley Fathers" to India.

Mrs. Hutchison, foundress of St. Catherine's Convent, Edinburgh.

The Baroness Von Hugel (née Farquharson), wife of the late Austrian Ambassador.

Colonel Holmes, late 89th Regiment.

Miss Hesketh, daughter of the late Sir Thomas Hesketh.

Captain Haycock.

Lieut.-Colonel Richard Holmes, 89th Regiment.

Mrs. Cashel Hoey.

Henry Hepburne. A Jesuit.

George Herbert, barrister-at-law, and Mrs. Herbert.

Miss Hartley, of Bayswater.

Miss Holdsworth.

Mrs. John Hamer, daughter of Charles Blake Allnatt, barrister-at-law.

Mrs. Houldsworth, of Craigforth, N.B.

I

Mrs. Inglefield, wife of Major Inglefield.

Mrs. Darcy Irvine, wife of Captain Darcy Irvine, R.N.

J

Rev. F. F. Jones, B.A., Pembroke College, Cambridge. A priest.

Rev. Henry James, M.A., Oxford; Vicar of St. Andrew's, Wells-street. A Jesuit.

Rev. J. Jerrard, D.C.L., late Fellow of Caius College, Cambridge, and Fellow and Examiner of London University.

Mrs. J. H. Jerrard, wife of Fellow and Examiner of London University.

J. H. Jones, Methodist Minister. A priest.

Arthur Johnson, Keble College, Oxford.

J. S. Johnstone, M.A., Oxford.

Rev. Henry Francis John Jones, B.A., Oxford, of Humpheston Hall, Salop.

Mrs. Owen Jones, wife of author of "The Grammar of Ornament."

Major Johnstone and the Misses Johnstone, of Folkestone.

Arthur Jackson, 6th Royal Regiment.

Mrs. Johnson, of Cross, wife of the Member for Exeter and daughter of Sir Theodore Brinckman, Bart.

Lady Hope-Johnstone.

Miss Alicia Hope-Johnstone.

H. James, barrister-at-law.

Sidney Joyce, Christ Church, Oxford.

Mrs. Coventry Jones.

Richard Jones, architect, Ryde, and Mrs. Jones.

J. R. Judge, barrister-at-law.

Dr. Alan Jennings, Mrs. Jennings, and family.

G. F. Johnson, son of late Consul at Antwerp, and Mrs. Johnson.

K

The late Countess of Kenmare.

Lord Nigel Kennedy.

Lord A. Kennedy.

Captain Edward Philip King-Salter.

Rev. T. H. King, Exeter College, Oxford; now a Solicitor.

Rev. J. Kynaston, Trinity College, Cambridge; now a Solicitor.

Rev. Lord Henry Francis Kerr, son of 6th Marquis of Lothian, K.T.; Rector of Dittisham, and J.P. for Devonshire.

Lord John Kerr.

Lady Cecil Kerr. A nun.

Lady Henry Kerr, daughter of Hon. Sir Alexander Hope, G.C.B.

William Kerr, son of Lord Henry Kerr. A Jesuit.

Henry Schomberg Kerr, son of Lord Henry Kerr. A Jesuit priest.

Francis Kerr, of Chiefswood, son of Lord Henry Kerr.

Lord Walter Talbot Kerr, R.N., son of 7th Marquis of Lothian.

Lady Amabel Kerr, daughter of 6th Earl Cowper.

Colonel Lord Ralph Kerr, 10th Hussars.

George R. Kingdon, Scholar of Trinity College, Cambridge. A Jesuit priest.

T. Francis Knox, B.A., Scholar of Trinity College, Cambridge; grandson of the Earl of Ranfurley. A priest of the oratory.

Lady Victoria Kirwan, daughter of 2nd Marquis of Hastings.

B. S. Knowles, son of Sheridan Knowles.

Stuart Knill.

Rev. J. H. Kirk. A priest.

Rev. W. H. Kelke, M.A., Brasenose College, Oxford; curate at Bedford Leigh; now a Barrister.

Lady Kilmaine.

Henry J. Karslake, cousin of Sir John Karslake, some time Attorney-General. A priest.

Charles J. Karslake, ditto. A priest.

Rev. C. H. Kennard, M.A., University College, Oxford, Curate of Newland, Malvern. A priest.

Rev. Samuel W. Küttner; Chaplain to the Bishop of Jerusalem.

Francis Kiernan, M.R.C.S.

Baroness Keating, daughter of Judge Keating.

Mrs. Charles Kent, author of "Evelyn Stuart," and other novels.

Captain Blakie Keith, 39th Regiment.

Mrs. Keon, daughter of Major Hawkes, and widow of the Hon. Miles Gerald Keon, Colonial Secretary at Bermuda.

Lucius Kelly, Barrister-at-Law.

Frederic Shakerley Kempe, of Richmond.

Rev. Reginald C. Kempe, Magdalen College, Oxford.

John G. Kenyon, B.A., S.C.L., Christ Church, Oxford; grandson of second Lord Kenyon. A Papal Zouave and Private Chamberlain to Pope Leo XIII.

Miss Louisa Kirby, daughter of the Rector of Mayfield.

Mr. and Mrs. T. Kerrich, Harleston House, Norfolk.

William Kent, R.N., only son of the late Captain W. Kent, R.N., and father of Charles Kent, poet and journalist.

Edward Stewart Knill.

L

Elizabeth, Marchioness of Londonderry.

William Lockhart, B.A., Exeter College, Oxford. A priest.

Mrs. and Miss Lockhart.

Cecil Chetwynd, Marchioness of Lothian.

Rev. W. H. Lewthwaite, M.A., Trinity College, Cambridge; Vicar of Clifford. A priest.

Rev. Francis Lascelles, B.A., Trinity College, Cambridge; Perpetual Curate of Merevale; now a Barrister-at-Law.

Frederick Lucas, B.A. (London); sometime M.P. for Meath, and Editor of the *Tablet*.

Edward Lucas, Herongate, Brentwood.

Owen Lewis, M.P.

Francis, 7th Duke of Leeds, who sat in the Commons as Marquis of Carmarthen.

Lord Alexander Gordon Lennox, son of 5th Duke of Richmond.

The Honourable William Towry Law, son of 1st Lord Ellenborough; Vicar of Harborne, and Chancellor of the Diocese of Bath and Wells.

The Honourable Mrs. William Towry Law.

Augustus H. Law, a Jesuit Missionary in South Africa.

Thomas Graves Law. A priest of the Oratory.

Helen Ann Law. Sister of mercy.

The Hon. Mrs. Charles Law.

Miss Elizabeth Law. A nun.

Mrs. Edmund Law.

Rev. D. Lewis, M.A., Fellow of Jesus College, and Curate of St. Mary the Virgin, Oxford.

Honourable Mrs. David Lewis, daughter of first Lord Methuen.

S. B. Lamb, Solicitor, London.

Honourable Colin Lindsay, son of 24th Earl of Crawford and Balcarres; President of the English Church Union.

Lady Frances Lindsay, daughter of 4th Earl of Wicklow.

William Leigh, J.P., D.C.L., of Woodchester Park, Gloucestershire.

Mrs. Caroline Leigh, daughter of Sir John G. Cottrell, Bart., M.P.

Rev. H. W. Lloyd, M.A., Scholar of Jesus College, Oxford.

Rev. Francis Henry Laing, Queen's College, Cambridge; Curate at Eglingham. A priest.

Rev. C. J. Laprimaudaye, M.A., St. John's College, Oxford; Rector of Lavington.

Mrs. Laprimaudaye, sister of Mr. Hubbard, M.P.; and Family.

W. W. Lander, Banker.

Robert Laing, Town Clerk of Jedburgh.

Henry Murray Lane, Chester Herald in Her Majesty's College of Arms.

Mrs. Murray Lane.

J. Leigh, Brasenose College, Oxford.

Mrs. Lewis, formerly Mrs. Spedding, of Lake Bank, Ambleside.

Mrs. Littledale, of Stoke Hill, Guildford.

H. G. Lumsden, of Clova and Auchindoir, Aberdeenshire.

Rev. William Lovell, M.A., Exeter College, Oxford; Curate at Wantage.

W. Y. Hinde-Lloyd.

E. Lumley, the publisher.

Captain Lawrence.

Alfred Le Mesurier, Oriel College, Oxford.

John Lister, B.A., Brasenose College, Oxford.

Rev. S. C. Lord, Rector of Farmborough.

Mrs. Lord.

Miss La Touche.

D. C. Lathbury, Brasenose College, Oxford.

Rev. Thos. S. Livius, M.A., Oriel College, Oxford; Curate of St. Kea, Cornwall. A priest.

W. S. Lilly, B.A., St. Peter's College, Cambridge: Barrister-at-Law.

Richard Wentworth Lambe, D.L., Durham.

The Lady Louth.

The Lady Lambert.

Alfred Lambart, grandson of the late Earl of Cavan.

Mrs. Leathley, wife of W. H. Leathley, Barrister-at-law; author of popular books for the young.

Mrs. Lance.

Mrs. Lean (née Bellingham), of Lyme Regis.

Miss Lethbridge, daughter of Sir Thomas Lethbridge.

William Lovell.

Stuart Lovell.

Charles Lovell.

Rev. A. Leeson.

Princess de Ligne, daughter of Sir David Cunyngham.

Rev. W. H. Littleboy, Curate at Shearston.

Mrs. Lamberh.

Augusta, Viscomtess de Lubersac, daughter of Rev. Percival Fyre, Rector of St. Winnow, Cornwall, formerly Vicar of Holy Trinity, Brompton.

Mrs. Lyall, wife of Rector of St. Dionis Backchurch.

Mrs. Richard Lamb.

Mrs. Owen Lewis, wife of the Member for Carlow.

W. E. Leslie, M.A., Oxford. A Jesuit.

Trevor Lloyd, M.A., Magdalen Hall, Oxford. A Jesuit.

Charles La Touche, of Marlay.

T. J. E. A. Lloyd, Magdalen Hall, Oxford.

The Misses Lloyd, of St. Mary Church, Torquay.

Miss Langston, foundress of an Anglican Sisterhood.

Charles J. Leslie.

F. Augustine Luck. A Benedictine priest.

Edmund J. Luck. A Benedictine priest.

Thomas Luck. A priest.

Mrs. Lambert.

Miss Flora Lavie.

Mrs. Linklater, wife of a clergyman.

Mrs. Locke, widow of Major Locke, son of General and Lady Matilda Locke.

H. G. Lawson, Wadham College, Oxford.

Mrs. and two Misses Leslie. Both nuns.

Mrs. Lloyd, daughter of the late Sir John Carden, Bart., and mother of Lady Rossmore.

Mrs. Lovell, niece of Sir Henry Bishop, the composer.

Miss Lambert, daughter of Sir George Lambert.

Miss Lyons, daughter of Captain Lyons, R.N.

John Cathcart Lees, brother of the late Sir Harcourt Lees, Bart.

Mr. and Mrs. Thomas Longueville, of Penyllan, Oswestry.

Mrs. Lynch, wife of Charles Lynch, J.P., Petersburg, Galway.

David Lambe. A priest.

Miss Lockyer, daughter of Captain Lockyer, R N.

Philip Limerick. A Dominican priest.

Cecil Bruce Lane.

Mrs. Charles Leveson Lane.

Mrs. Lucas, wife of Captain Lucas.

Mrs. Lucas, mother of Frederick Lucas, sometime Member of co. Meath.

Mrs. Le Mesurier and the Misses Le Mesurier.

Miss Alice Lees, granddaughter of the Rev. Sir Harcourt Lees, Bart., Black Rock House, co. Dublin.

Marquise de Labedoyère, daughter of Lord Greville.

The Misses Lamprell, daughters of Captain T. G. Lamprell.

Mr. and Mrs. Archibald Leslie.

M

Henry Edward Manning, Fellow of Merton College, Oxford; Rector of Lavington, Archdeacon of Chichester. Cardinal Archbishop of Westminster.

Charles J. Manning, the Cardinal's brother.

Mrs. C. J. Manning, eldest daughter of Rev. Sir Augustus Brydges Henniker, Bart.

The late Mrs. Charles Manning.

W. H. Manning. A Priest and Monsignor.

Rev. Henry Marshall, M.A., Pembroke College, Oxford ; Curate at Burton Agnes. A priest.

Richard Mills, Brasenose College, Oxford ; Solicitor.

The Right Honourable Lord Robert Montagu, M.A., Trinity College, Cambridge, P.C., M.P., son of the sixth Duke of Manchester.

Lady Robert Montagu.

Rev. W. Maskell, M.A., University College, Oxford ; Examining Chaplain to the Bishop of Exeter.

C. R. Scott Murray, Christ Church, Oxford, Danesfield ; some time M.P. for Buckinghamshire.

The Viscountess Maidstone, daughter of Sir George Jenkinson, Bart., M.P.

Rev. T. W. Marshall, Trinity College, Cambridge ; Vicar of Swallowcliffe ; author of " Christian Missions."

Mr. and Mrs. John Matthews.

Rev. Richard Gell Macmullen, M.A. ; Fellow of Corpus Christi College, and Vicar of St. Mary Magdalen's, Oxford. A priest and canon.

Rev. John Brande Morris, M.A. ; Fellow of Exeter College, Oxford. A priest.

James Arthur V. Maude, late 77th Regiment, and nephew of Lord Hawarden. A priest of the Oratory.

Rev. W. T. Moberley ; Curate of Easton, Winchester.

Rev. Sir Paul Molesworth, Bart., M.A., Trinity College, Cambridge ; formerly Rector of Tetcott, Devon.

Lady Molesworth.

Rev. Frederick G. Maples, B.A., St. John's College, Cambridge ; Curate of St. Mary's, Soho. A priest.

Rev. Clement Harington Moore, M.A., Christ Church ; Curate of St. Barnabas, Oxford. A priest.

Henry Austin Mills, Trinity College, Cambridge. A priest.

Rev. Robert Sadleir Moody, M.A., and Mrs. Moody.

Rev. James R. Madan, M.A., Queen's College, Oxford ; Head of Protestant Missionary College at Warminster. A priest.

Robert Monteith of Carstairs, M.A., Trinity College, Cambridge.

Rev. Thomas Meyrick, M.A. ; Scholar of Corpus Christi, First Class in Classics, Oxford. A Jesuit.

Rev. John G. MacLeod, M.A., Exeter College, Oxford. A Jesuit.

John Morris, Trinity College, Cambridge, author of " Troubles of our Catholic Forefathers." A Jesuit.

Wilfrid Mordaunt. A Jesuit.

Rev. T. Minster, M.A., St. Catherine's College, Cambridge. Vicar of St. Saviour's, Leeds.

Rev. G. Montgomery, M.A., Trinity College, Dublin, Curate at Castleknock. A priest.

Honourable Mrs. Marmaduke Constable Maxwell.

J. Reynell Morell, of the British Museum.

Algernon Moore, University College, London. A priest.

Rev. Arthur Marshall ; Curate at Liverpool. Author of " Comedy of Convocation."

Mrs. McChristie, wife of the City Revising Barrister.

Admiral Russell Henry Manners, F.R.S., of the Rutland family.

Mrs. Manners and Miss Manners.

Edwin R. Martin. A priest.

Lady Agnes Murray, of Polmaise.

Mrs. Miller, Panmure House, Forfarshire.

Rev. Henry Morland, B.A., Hertford College, Oxford ; Curate of Middle Claydon. A priest.

Rev. Philip G. Munro. A priest.

W. C. Maude, Exeter College, Oxford.

Mrs. Arthur Maude.

Rev. Arthur Mayo, Victoria Cross, late Indian Navy, B.A., Magdalen Hall, Oxford.

Mrs. Arthur Mayo.

Miss Maitland, daughter of Rev. J. Maitland, D.D., a J.P. and D.L. for Kirkcudbrightshire ; and granddaughter of the Hon. Mrs. Bellamy Gordon, of Kenmure.

Sir Archibald Keppel McDonald, Bart.

The late Lady Murray, Philiphaugh.

John Murray, eldest son of Sir John Murray, Bart., of Philiphaugh.

Mrs. John Murray.

Rev. A. H. Mathews, B.A. A priest.

The Hon. Mrs. Alfred Montgomery, daughter of Lord Leconfield, and author of " On the Wing."

Professor St. George Mivart.

The Lady Milford, daughter of third Earl of Wicklow.

Mrs. Mainwaring.

Mrs. Melhuish.

The late Charles Moore, of Mooresfort, Tipperary, sometime M.P., and father of Arthur Moore, M.P.

A. N. L. McCaul, Magdalen College, Oxford. An Oratorian.

Frank Marshall, dramatic author.

L. M. Mackenzie, B.A., Exeter College, Oxford.

General McGowan, famous during the Sepoy Rebellion.

Captain Mitchell, of Buldaire and Balfour.

Rev. H. R. Meakinson.

Rev. James Marshall, Curate of St. Bartholomew's, Moor Lane.

Rev. H. Milner, Curate of Barnoldswick.

Rev. T. Moyston, an Irish Vicar.

Rev. A. Meers, Isle of Man.

Rev. J. Maphson, Curate of St. Mary's, Soho.

Rev R. Moore, Missionary of the Society for the Propagation of the Gospel in India.

A. Morgan, Librarian of Walsall.

Francis Moreton, eldest son of Captain the Hon. Percy Moreton and grandson of the 1st Earl of Ducie.

Major MacKenzie.

Mrs. Mends, wife of the late Captain G. P. Mends, R.N.

Ernest Marras.

Rev. W. C. Monro, Curate of St. Paul's, Knightsbridge.

Mrs. Monro and two children.

Miss Munro, of Seymour Street.

Miss Mallet, daughter of the late Hugh Mallet, of Ash House, North Devon.

Mr. and Mrs. Marriage, Quakers.

Mrs. J. Mill Muldary (formerly Gun Cuninghame), niece of the late Earl of Limerick.

Rev. Frederick Myers. A Jesuit.

Charles John Henry Massingberd-Mundy, South Ormsby Hall, Lincolnshire.

Miss McGee, daughter of Chaplain at Gibraltar. A nun.

Mrs. Merewether, widow of Dean of Hereford.

The Misses Merewether, daughters of the late Dean of Hereford.

John Merewether, Christ Church, Oxford.

G. L. Gordon Milne, son of the Incumbent of St. James's, Cupar, Fife.

Mrs. Gordon Milne, widow of the Incumbent.

J. F. Gordon Milne, first officer of the ship "British Duke."

Dr. Moir, Edinburgh.

J. Miller, Edinburgh, publisher.

Mrs. Oliver Miller, of Dundee.

Rev. W. C. A. MacLaurin, Dean of Elgin.

Mrs. McLaurin.

Julius McLaurin, late Professor of Mathematics at Stoneyhurst.

Miss Murray, Anglican Sister at Oxford.

Major Laing Meason, late 8th Hussars.

Miss Laing Meason. A nun.

The Hon. Mrs. Laing Meason.

Malcolm Laing Meason, journalist and author; late 10th Hussars.

Mrs. M. Laing Meason.

A. Laing Meason. A Jesuit.

Major-General Macmullen.

Mrs. Macmullen and children.

Rev. H. J. Marshall, D.D., Pembroke College, Oxford. A priest.

George B. Maycock, of Edgbaston, Birmingham.

Mrs. Mack, of Paston Hall, Norfolk.

Mrs. Martin, widow of Major Martin.

Miss Morgan, Bridgend, Glamorganshire.

W. Malpass. A priest.

Miss Maclean and Miss Louisa Maclean, daughters of the late Sir L. Munro Maclean.

Mrs. Middleton and Miss Middleton. A nun.

Rev. W. Murray, Incumbent at Colchester.

Miss Barbara Martin, daughter of Captain George Bohun Martin, R.N.

Mrs. Mills, wife of a Cornish clergyman.

Miss Mathew, now Countess della Marmora.

Miss Wykeham-Martin and Miss Alice Wykeham-Martin, daughters of Rev. R. Martin, of Leeds Castle, Kent.

W. H. Moore, surgeon, Woodbridge; his wife and family.

Charles E. MacDougall, son of Hon. Mr. Justice MacDougall.

Mrs. C. E. MacDougall, daughter of Colonel J. Jackson, Madras Army.

N

John Henry Newman, Fellow of Oriel College, and Vicar of St. Mary the Virgin, Oxford; Superior of the Birmingham Oratory.

The Duchess of Norfolk.

The Dowager Duchess of Norfolk.

Hon. Charles Horatio Nelson, son of 3rd Earl Nelson.

Rev. F. J. New, M.A., St. John's College, Oxford; Curate of Christ Church, St. Pancras.

Francis Thomas New, solicitor.

Mrs. F. T. New, cousin of the late Bishop Selwyn and of the late Lord Justice Selwyn.

Colonel Selwyn New, late of Madras Army.

Mortimer New.

Hon. Wm. North, son of Baroness North, Life Guards; heir apparent to Barony of North.

Rev. A. Newdigate, Vicar of Kirk Hallam, and cousin of Mr. Newdegate, M.P.

William Payne Neville, M.A., Trinity College, Oxford. A priest.

Rev. David Charles Nicols, M.A., St. Peter's College, Cambridge; Curate at All Saint's, Margaret Street.

Rev. F. R. Neve, M.A., Oriel College, Oxford; Vicar of Poole Keynes. A priest and canon.

Richard Neave, of the War Office.

Rev. J. Spencer Northcote, M.A., Scholar of Corpus Christi College, Oxford, and First Class in Classics; Curate at Ilfracombe. A priest and canon.

The Lord Norreys, son and heir of the Earl of Abingdon.

The Countess Dowager of Newburgh.

Rev. W. Hayes Neligan, Curate of St. Margaret's, Leicester. A priest.

Ralph H. C. Nevile, Trinity Coll., Cam., of Wellingore Hall, Grantham.

Capt. Iltid Nicholl, R.N., second son of the late Right Hon. John Nicholl, M.P.

Lieut. Ernest Nightingale, son of the Baronet.

Rev. Geo. B. Norman, M.A., Trinity Coll., Cam.; Curate of Wooton.

Rev. Willis Nevins, Curate of St. Jude's, Southsea; author of various works.

Mrs. Willis Nevins.

Rev. T. N. Norton, Curate at Devizes.

Rev. H. Nelson, Curate at Frome Selwood.

Honourable Mrs. North.

Henry Norris. A priest.

Mrs. Stafford Northcote.

Captain Nesbitt, late of Royal Artillery.

Miss Greville Nugent, granddaughter of the Marquis of Westmeath.

Rev. Francis H. Nash, A.M., son of Rev. Dr. Nash.

Mrs. F. H. Nash.

William Nicholson, late Major 3rd Royal Lancashire Militia.

O

Rev. Lord Francis Godolphin Osborne, M.A., Cambridge; Rector of Elm, Frome, son of 8th Duke of Leeds

Rev. R. B. Osborne, Vicar of Dunston, son of "S. G. O."

Rev. Frederick Oakeley, M.A., Fellow of Balliol College, Select Preacher and Public Examiner at the University of Oxford; Minister of All Saint's, Margaret Street. A priest and canon.

William Wilfrid Oates, publisher.

Rev. Henry Nutcomb Oxenham, M.A., Scholar of Balliol College, Oxford.

The Earl of Orford.

Rev. R. Ornsby, M.A., Fellow of Trinity College, Oxford, First Class in Classics; Curate at Chichester.

Sebastian Okeley, M.A., Scholar of Trinity College, Cambridge; University Travelling Bachelor.

Rev. James Orr, B.A., Oriel College, Oxford.

Rev. George Oldham, M.A., Trinity College, Cambridge; Curate at Dorking. A priest; built St. Mary Magdalen's at Brighton.

Rev. Jas. O'Brien, M.A., Sidney Sussex Col., Cam., V. Lyneham. A priest.

Mrs. O Brien, wife of J. H. Archer O'Brien, M.R.I.A.

The late John Oxenford, dramatic author and critic of the *Times*.

William Eddowes Owen, M.A., son of a Protestant Canon. A priest.

Rev. M. O'Connor, an Irish Rector.

The Countess of Orford.

Mrs. Denis O'Conor, wife of M.P. for County Sligo, and daughter of Rev. W. Kevill-Davies of Croft Castle, Hertfordshire.

Mrs. Daniel O'Connell, wife of late M.P. for Tralee.

Mr. and Mrs. G. S. Ottywell, Baptists.

Miss Alice O Hanlon, of Manchester.

Mrs. Oddie, of Colney House, Herts.

Misses Georgiana and Katherine Oddie, nuns.

Arthur, Claude, and Philip Oddie.

Captain H. Oddie, 15th Regiment.

Mrs. Owen, wife of a Protestant canon.

Octavius Owen.

Mrs. O'Flaherty, widow of Anthony O'Flaherty, formerly M.P. for Galway.

Mrs. O'Grady, of Onslow Square.

Miss Agnes and Miss Lætitia Oliver, cousins of the late Bishop Selwyn.

Mrs. O'Mahony, wife of E. W. O'Mahony, barrister-at-law, daughter of Colonel Peisley L'Estrange, and sister-in-law of the Most Rev. Marcus Beresford, Protestant Archbishop of Armagh and Primate of Ireland.

P

Major-General Patterson.

Rev. James Laird Patterson, M.A., Trinity College, Curate of St. Thomas, Oxford. A priest and monsignor.

Professor Paley, M.A., St. John's College, Cambridge, grandson of the author of the "Evidences."

Miss Peel, sister of Sir Lawrence Peel.

Coventry Patmore, author of "The Angel in the House."

L. D. Powles, Barrister-at-Law.

Rev. Thomas Alder Pope, M.A., Jesus College, Cambridge; Rector of St. Matthias, Stoke Newington. A priest of the Birmingham Oratory.

Rev. R. V. Pope, B.A., London; Missionary of the S.P.G. in India. Now Master at the Oratory School, Birmingham.

Mrs. Pittar, author of "Conversion by my Bible and Prayer-book."

Rev. T. G. Pearse, B.A., Cambridge.

Rev. Daniel Parsons, M.A., Oriel College, Oxford.

Mrs. Parsons, authoress.

Rev. J. H. Pye, M.A., Trinity College, Cambridge, Rector of Clifton Campville. Now a Barrister-at-Law.

Mrs. H. J. Pye, daughter of the late Bishop Wilberforce.

Rev. William Palmer, M.A., Fellow of Magdalen College, and elder brother of Lord Selborne.

Augustus Welby Pugin, the reviver of Gothic Architecture in England.

Miss Adelaide Anne Procter, the poetess.

Wellesley Prendergast.

F. R. Wegg-Prosser, B.A., Balliol College, Oxford, Deputy-Lieutenant, J.P., and some time M.P. for Hertfordshire.

Edward Purbrick, Christ Church, Oxford. A Jesuit, and Rector of Stonyhurst College.

James Purbrick, Christ Church, Oxford, solicitor. A Jesuit.

Rev. J. Hungerford Pollen, M.A., Fellow of Merton College, Oxford, and now of South Kensington Museum; and Mrs. Pollen.

Sir Richard Hungerford Pollen, Bart.

Rev. W. G. Penny, M.A., Christ Church, Oxford, Vicar of Askenden. A priest.

Professor Pepper, of the Polytechnic.

F. H. Pownall, son of Henry Pownall, J.P. of Spring-grove.

Rev. T. B. Parkinson, M.A., Queen's College, Cambridge; Incumbent of St. Mary's, Wakefield. A Jesuit.

W. Z. Palmer, M.A., Oxford.

J. O'Fallon Pope, M.A., Christ Church, Oxford. A Jesuit.

Henry Watson Parker, solicitor.

Harriet Elizabeth, sister of the late Sir Joseph Peacock, Bart.

Rev. J. Plumer, M.A., Balliol College, Oxford, son of the late Master of the Rolls.

Mrs. Priestman, of Benwell House, near Newcastle-on-Tyne.

Rev. William Pope, B.A., Christ's College, Cambridge, curate near Bolton. A priest.

The Hon. Captain Pakenham, of the Guards, nephew of the Duke of Wellington and Equerry of the Queen. A Passionist.

Miss Prestwich, sister of Professor Prestwich, F.R.S.

Miss Pritchard, daughter of the Rev. Professor Pritchard. A nun.

John Philp, publisher.

Rev. J. A. Poole, B.A., Curate of St. John's, Miles Platting, Lancashire.

Miss Plues, Superior of Ladies' Home, Kensington Square.

John Procter, a Quaker.

Mrs. C. Prichard.

The late Countess of Portarlington, daughter of 3rd Marquis of Londonderry, and sister-in-law of the Duke of Marlborough.

Robert B. Phillips, M.A., Trinity Col., Oxford, D.L., of Longworth, Hereford.

Rev. Ch. E. Parry, B.A. A priest.

The Hon. Esther Pomeroy, sister of Viscount Harberton.

Rev. H. M. Parker, M.A., Lincoln College, Oxford; Curate of St. Bartholomew's, Brighton.

Colonel Lenox Prendergast.

Mrs. Lenox Prendergast, daughter of Neil Malcolm.

A. R. Pryor, B.A., University College, Oxford.

Charles F. Palmer, author of "History of Tamworth" and "Life of Cardinal Howard." A Dominican priest.

Edward Powell, Scholar of Magdalen College, Oxford.

J. O. Halliwell-Phillips.

Captain C. C. Pye.

J. S. Smyth-Pigott, Brockley Hall.

Alfred C. Smyth-Pigott, Brockley Hall.

W. E. Poynter, B.A., Queen's College, Cambridge.

F. A. Pope, Wadham College, Oxford.

Charles Henry Poole, B.L., St Alban Hall, Oxford.

Miss Pope, Miss L. Pope, and Miss E. Pope. All nuns.

Admiral Peirse.

Miss Clara Phillpotts, granddaughter of late Bishop of Exeter.

Miss Palk.

Owen Philips, Trinity Coll., Cambridge.

Captain Pearse, R.N., Devonport.

John O. Payne, M.A., St. Peter's College, Cambridge; Curate at Linslade, Bucks.

A. G. Payne, B.A., St. Peter's College, Cambridge.

Dr. and Mrs. Penrice.

Mrs. Pybus and family.

Mrs. Coventry Patmore, daughter of Sir John Byles, the judge.

Captain W. Prentis, late Scots Greys.

William Purdue, architect.

Mrs. Paravacini, wife of Bursar of Balliol College, Oxford.

The Lady Elizabeth Peat, niece of Sir Walter Scott.

Miss Emily Peel, niece of Sir Laurence Peel.

Edward Peacock, F.S.A., Bottesford Manor, Lincoln.

Henrietta, daughter of Sir T. Phillips, Bart.

Charles Parfitt. Priest and monsignor.

F. Potter, M.A., Merton College, Oxford; son of Member for Rochdale.

Miss Edith Potter, daughter of the Member for Rochdale.

Miss Pennell, daughter of Admiral Pennell.

Captain Pauli, R.N., now in the Consular Service.

Mrs. Partridge, widow of the late Dr. Partridge, of Brook-street, Grosvenor-square; her two sons and a daughter.

Lucy, wife of Rev. G. P. Phillips and sister of Dr. Vaughan, Master of the Temple.

Rev. G. Phillips, nephew of Dr. Vaughan. A priest.

Miss Gertrude Phillips, niece of Dr. Vaughan. A nun.

Mrs. R. V. Pope, niece of Dr. Vaughan.

Miss Amy Pope, daughter of W. H. Pope, Judge in Prince Edward's Island.

Edward Plater, of the War Office.

J. R. Poole, solicitor.

Mrs. J. Ruscomb Poole.

The Misses Poole.

Mrs. Powell, daughter of Captain John Lumsden, of Clova, Aberdeenshire.

Dr. Peart, J.P., Kildare.

William Pigott, solicitor, Portarlington.

Miss Piggott, authoress.

Lieutenant-Colonel Palmer, Alnwick.

W. F. Paul, of the Colonial Service.

Edmund Peel, nephew of Sir Lawrence Peel.

William Peel, ditto.

The Misses Perceval, daughters of a clergyman. One of them a nun.

Mrs. Pratt, daughter of Sir John Lethbridge, Bart.

Mrs. Purcell, daughter of Sir John Lethbridge, Bart.

Mrs. Pugin, widow of Augustus Welby Pugin, architect.

Mrs. R. Lyndsey Dillon Purcell.

Robert Priest, St. Augustine's College, Canterbury.

George Godfrey Place, barrister-at-law, Dublin.

Mrs. Prickett, wife of Colonel Prickett, of Boreas Hill, near Hull, and daughter of the late Sir Charles Dodsworth.

Mr. Plummer, solicitor, Falmouth, and Mrs. Plummer.

Mr. and Mrs. De la Pole.

Mrs. Croker Pennell, daughter of late Sir William Follett.

Q

Caroline, Marchioness of Queensberry.

R

The Marquis of Ripon.

The Honourable Mrs. David Ross, of Bladensberg, daughter of Ninth Viscount Massareene and Ferrard, and Miss Ross.

Edmund F. T. Ross of Bladensberg, Royal Engineers.

John Ross of Bladensberg, Coldstream Guards.

Hon. Mrs. John Ross of Bladensberg, daughter of 10th Viscount Massareene and Ferrard.

Robert S. Ross of Bladensberg, M.A., Exeter College; barrister-at-law. A Jesuit.

G. Elliot Ranken, B.A., Scholar of University College, Oxford; formerly Captain, Royal Glamorgan Artillery. Private Chamberlain to late and present Pope.

Rev. Martin Luther Rule, B.A., Pembroke College, Cambridge, Curate at Brighton. Son of Dr. Rule, Wesleyan Minister.

Rev. Henry Augustus Rawes, M.A., Trinity College, Cambridge. A priest.

Rev. George Rose, M.A., reader at the Temple Church, and since known as "Arthur Sketchley."

William W. Roberts, M.A., Oxford. A priest.

Rev. Walter Croke Robinson, M.A., Fellow of New College, Oxford. A priest.

James Boon Rowe, St. John's College, Cambridge. A priest of the Oratory.

Rev. Seton P. Rooke, M.A., Oriel College, Oxford; Curate of St. Saviour's, Leeds. A Dominican priest.

Rev. E. Ransford, St. John's College, Cambridge.

M. J. Rhodes, M.A., Trinity College, Cambridge.

John Edmund Reade, author of poems.

Mrs. J. E. Reade, niece of Sir John Chandos Reade, Bart.

P. Le Page Renouf, Pembroke College, Oxford, H.M. Inspector of Schools.

Rev. M. Watts Russell, M.A., Christ Church, Oxford; Vicar of Benefield; Ilam Hall, Staffordshire. A priest.

M. Watts Russell, jun. A Passionist.

Rev. T. C. Robertson, Chaplain to Duke of Buccleuch.

Rev. George Dudley Ryder, M.A., Oriel College, Oxford; son of Bishop of Lichfield, and grandson of the Earl of Harrowby.

Henry Ignatius Dudley Ryder. A priest.

Cyril Ryder. A priest.

Charles E. Ryder. A priest.

George Lisle Ryder, of the Treasury.

James Burton Robertson, author of various philosophical works.

Thomas Rawlinson, M.A., brother of Sir Henry Rawlinson.

W. J. B. Richards, St. Mary Hall, Oxford. A priest.

G. J. Richards, St. Mary Hall, Oxford.

Mrs. Howard Rice, wife of Vicar of
. Sutton Courtney.
Stephen Ram, D.L., of Ramsfort, Gorey.
Rev. Richard E. Rann, B.A., Queen's
College, Oxford, Vicar of Thatcham,
Berks.
Lieutenant Randolph, R.N.
John Henry Röhrs, Fellow of Jesus Col-
lege, Cambridge.
Arthur Russell, son of Rev. A. B. Rus-
sell, Rector of Laverton. A priest.
F. Peel Round, B.A., Balliol College,
Oxford; Gentleman Usher of the Green
Rod.
Sir Percival Radcliffe, Bart.
T. A. Robinson, Corpus Christi, Oxford;
Lieutenant in the Artillery.
H. L. Reader, B.A., Merton College, Ox-
ford. A priest and Carthusian.
Frederick W. Ratcliff, Birmingham.
Joseph Redman; formerly a lay worker at
St. Peter's, London Docks. A priest.
Mrs. Routh, wife of the Rector of Tile-
hurst.
Rev. F. Remington, B.A., Cambridge,
Curate at Folkestone; his wife and his
sister.
Rev. W. H. Ratcliffe, Curate of St. Mary
Magdalen's, Paddington.
Mrs. Radley, of Lambate Grange.
Rev. E. Randolph, M.A., Jesus College,
Cambridge; Vicar of St. Clement's,
Cambridge.
Mrs. E. Randolph and family.
Rev. C. R. Rowlatt, Curate at Grays
Thurrock.
Rev. Charles George Ramsey.
W. H. Roberts, M.A., Cambridge, D.L.,
Recorder of Grantham.
Miss Neville Rolfe.
W. S. Rockstro.
Mrs. and Miss Rose.
Sir Arthur Rumbold, Bart.
W. M. J. Ring. A priest.
Miss Rivaz.
Miss Rokeby, of Arthingworth Manor
House, Northamptonshire.
Miss Rudsdell and Miss Mary Rudsdell,
daughters of Sir Joseph Rudsdell,
K.C.M.G., Grenadier Guards.
Miss M. Roberts, daughter of the late
W. Roberts, of Harborne Hall.
R. Richardson, Priest of the Order of
Charity.
George Richardson, solicitor, Manchester.
Miss Ross, of Edge Hill, Liverpool.
Mr. and Mrs. Reginald Reynolds.
John Roberts, of the War Office.
Denham Robinson, of the War Office.
Mr. Rolph, of the War Office.
Mrs. and the Misses Watts Russell.
Miss Rogers, daughter of the late Francis
Newman Rogers, Q.C., Recorder of
Exeter.

Captain Rayner, late 5th Royal Lancashire
Militia.
Captain Godfrey E. A. Radcliffe, brother
of Sir J. P. Radcliffe, Bart.
The Misses Rodwell, daughters of the
Rector of Ethelburga's. One of them
a Carmelite nun.
Humphrey Ravenscroft, of Lincoln's Inn.
Mr. and Mrs. David P. Watts Russell.
Miss Louisa Radcliffe, of Morehampton
House, Donnybrook.
S. H. Rowson. A priest.

S

The Rev. Orby Shipley.
Mrs. Shipley.
Rev. John R. Shortland, M.A., Oriel
College, Oxford, Curate at Kibworth
Beauchamp. A priest and canon.
S. N. Stokes, B.A., Scholar of Trinity
College, Cambridge; H.M. Inspector of
Schools.
Mrs. S. N. Stokes.
C. S. Stokes, Trinity College, Cambridge.
Hon. and Rev. George Spencer, son of
2nd Earl Spencer, K.G., and Chaplain
to Bishop Blomfield of London. A
Passionist priest.
Mrs. Slade, wife of General Slade.
Sir William Stewart, Bart., of Murthley.
Rev. Charles Seager, M.A., Worcester
College; Assistant Professor of Hebrew
at Oxford.
Charles Seager, jun. A priest.
J. R. Hope-Scott, M.A., Fellow of
Merton College, Oxford, Q.C., D.C.L.
Mrs. Hope-Scott, granddaughter of Sir
Walter Scott.
Rev. Ambrose St. John, M.A., Christ
Church, Oxford; curate at East Farleigh.
A priest of the Oratory.
Rev. Edward Gifford Shapcote, B.A.,
Christi College, Cambridge, Curate of
St. George-in-the-East.
The late Sir John Simeon, Bart, M.P.
The Hon. Dowager Lady Simeon.
Miss Surtees, Hamsterley Hull, Durham.
Rev. Richard Waldo Sibthorpe, B.D.,
Fellow of Magdalen College, Oxford;
Incumbent at Ryde. A priest.
Rev. John Campbell Smith, M.A., Cam-
bridge.
Reginald Schomberg, Barrister-at-law.
William Simpson, Trinity College, Cam-
bridge; Lord of the Manor of Mitcham,
and a descendant of Archbishop Cran-
mer.
Robert Simpson, St. John's College,
Oxford. A priest.
Rev. Richard Simpson, M.A., Oriel
College, Oxford; vicar of Mitcham.
Mrs. Richard Simpson, née Cranmer.
Miss Emily Simpson. A nun.

Edward Swainson, Trinity College, Cambridge. A priest.

Rev. R. Stanton, B.A., Brasenose College, Oxford. A priest of the Oratory.

Rev. Bernard Smith, Fellow of Magdalen College, Oxford, Vicar of Leadenham. A priest and canon.

Edward Scargill, Queen's College, Cambridge. Wrangler.

John Stephens, Trinity College, Cambridge.

Rev. Thomas Scratton, M.A., Christ Church, Oxford, Curate at Benson. A priest.

J. J. Saint, B.A., Christ Church, Oxford, Recorder of Newark.

Miss Stanley, daughter of Bishop Stanley of Norwich and sister of the Dean of Westminster.

J. Simpson, M.A., Scholar of Trinity College, Cambridge. A priest.

Rev. Robt. K. Sconce, B.A., Brasenose College, Oxford.

Rev. Jas. A. Stewart, M.A., St. John's College, Camb., Rector of Vange, Essex; his son and daughter.

W. Clement Scott, journalist and dramatic author.

Captain F. Shelton, late 93rd Highlanders. Mrs. Shelton.

J. P. H. Wyndham Spedding, Whitehaven, Trinity College, Cambridge.

C. J. Moncrieff Smyth, Christ's College, Cambridge. A priest.

Rev. Edwin Trevelyan Smith, M.A., St. John's College, Camb., Vicar of Cannock.

Mrs. Edwin Trevelyan Smith, sister of late Rev. J. Riddell, M.A., Fellow and Tutor of Balliol College, Oxford.

Sir John Sutton, Bart.

Mr. and Mrs. Schenk, of Brighton.

Miss Statter, daughter of Vicar of Worminghall.

Rev. James Scratton, M.A., St. John's College, Cambridge, Curate at Sittingbourne. A priest.

The Misses Somerville, daughters of the celebrated Mrs. Somerville.

Arthur John Shelley, nephew of the late Sir John Shelley, Bart., M.P. for Westminster.

Mr. and Mrs. John Stewart, of Ballechin. Marmaduke Sellon.

Charles Sellon.

Rev. J. Hansom Sperling, Rector of Westbourne, Sussex.

Mrs. Sperling and family.

Rev. James Stewart, M.A., Trinity College, Cambridge; Curate of Wolverstone, Professor at the Catholic University of Ireland.

H. Stevenson.

F. A. Sass, M.R.C.D.

Edward A. Selle. A priest.

Christopher Scott. Priest and canon.

Alexander B. Shea, barrister-at-law.

Mrs. Alexander B. Shea.

Rev. Fenwick Skrimshire, son of late Rector of Hertford. A priest.

Mrs. H. Fenwick Skrimshire, wife of late Rector of Hertford, five sons and two daughters.

Rev. Thomas Stephens, Vicar of Rathersage.

Philip Serle, Balliol College, Oxford.

Rev. J. A. Stothert, Episcopal Church of Scotland.

Rev. W. A. Scott, Rector near Birmingham.

Rev. James Hy. Shepperd, M.A., Queen's College, Oxford.

Miss Fanny Lillias Samler, daughter of the late Major Samler.

Dr. and Mrs. Shepherd, of Richmond.

Mrs. Story, wife of Admiral Story, R.N.

E. E. Sass, M.D., and Mrs. Sass.

Joseph Stevenson, M.A., Durham. A Jesuit.

Sir Andrew Smith, K.C.B.

Captain John Ramsay Slade, R.H.A.

Mrs. J. Somervell, granddaughter of the Earl of Camperdown.

Rev. Parks Smith, M.A., Vicar of St. John's, Torquay.

Mrs. Stewart, wife of Colonel Stewart of Folkestone, and Miss Alice Stewart, Sisters of St. Catherine's Anglican Convent, Folkestone.

Miss Eliza Allen Starr, authoress.

Lady Anne Sherson, sister of the Marquis of Townshend.

Mr. and Mrs. Geoffrey St. Aubyn.

Lieutenant St. Andrew St. John, R.N.

Mrs. St. Andrew St. John.

Rev. Joseph Searle. A priest.

Edward Stillwell, late of the War Office.

Mrs. Edward Stillwell.

Dr. Shears of Streatham.

Miss Frances Sidebottom, daughter of a clergyman.

Thomas H. Shaw, author of " Reasons for Returning to the True Fold."

Sydney F. Smith. A Jesuit.

Mr. George Lynch Staunton.

Superior and six Sisters of St. Mary's Protestant Priory, Hackney. All now Catholic nuns.

Miss Fanny A. Seymour, daughter of G. E. Seymour, of Forest Hill, Windsor.

Frances, sister of Sir Richard Sutton, Bart.

Francis Sutton, of Revell Grange, Sheffield.

Mrs. Walter Shirley.

Miss Margaret Speid, of Forneth.

Miss Soames, of Irnham Hall, Grantham.

Philip Shepheard, M.D., and the Misses Shepheard.

Mr. and Mrs. Rutherford Smith.

Miss Stuart, Anglican Sister at Oxford.

Lieutenant Thomas Say, Bombay Army; his wife, daughter, and two sons.

Captain H. N. R. Storks, late 9-th Regiment.

Miss Spicer, of Spy Park, Wiltshire.

Mr. and Mrs. Sydney Savory.

Major John Sewell. A Jesuit.

Mr. and Mrs. George Stanley.

Miss Smith, daughter of an Essex vicar.

Miss Murray Stewart.

William Shapter, son of Dr. Shapter of Exeter. A Jesuit.

Miss Shapter. A Poor Clare.

Mrs. Spearman, daughter-in-law of the Right Hon. Sir A. Y. Spearman, Bart.

A. St. John Seally, Lieutenant H.M.'s Artillery Militia, grandson of Rev. John Seally, LL.D.

Mrs. A. St. John Seally, with three sons and three daughters.

Edward Scholefield, brother of M.P. for Birmingham.

Robert Shuttleworth, M.D.

William Sankey, M.A., Trinity College, Cambridge.

Mrs. William Sankey, two sons and two daughters.

Robert Sutton Swabey, organist and composer.

Mrs. Colonel Simmonds, daughter of Sir Robert Graham, Bart.

William Henry and Robert Graham Simmonds, sons of above.

A. P. Skene, Durham University.

Mrs. Sutcliffe, wife of the late Director of Public Instruction, Bengal.

T

Hon. and Rev. George Talbot, M.A., Balliol College, Oxford, son of 3rd Baron Talbot de Malahide, and vicar of Evercreech, Somersetshire. A priest and monsignor.

Hon. Gilbert Chetwynd Talbot, Fellow of Balliol College, Oxford, son of 2nd Earl Talbot, and uncle of the present Earl of Shrewsbury. A priest and monsignor.

T. J. Thompson, Trinity College, Camb.; father of painter of the "Roll Call."

Mrs. T. J. Thompson.

Miss Elizabeth Thompson, painter of the "Roll Call."

Miss Alice Christiana Gertrude Thompson, author of "Preludes."

Rev. Lord Charles Thynne, M.A., Christ Church, Oxford, son of 2nd Earl of Bath, vicar of Longbridge, rector of

Kingston Deverell, and canon Canterbury.

Lady Charles Thynne, daughter of Right Rev. R. Bagot, Bishop of Bath and Wells.

J. W. N. Townsend, of Clifton. A priest.

Rev. Edward Healy Thompson, M.A., Emmanuel College, Cambridge; Curate of St James's, Piccadilly.

Stephen Taylor, barrister-at-law.

Rev. W. G. Todd, M.A., Trinity College, Dublin; Curate of St. James', Bristol. A priest and canon.

Rev. Reginald Tuke.

Rev. William Tylee, B.A., Oriel College, Oxford. A priest.

General Tylee.

Mrs. Tylee, wife of General Tylee.

Rev. Gordon Thompson, M.A., Scholar of Sidney Sussex College, Cambridge.

George Tickell, M.A., Fellow of University College, Oxford. A Jesuit missionary in the West Indies.

Rev. C. Thomas, B.A., Exeter College, Oxford.

Rev. F. W. Trenow, St. John's College, Oxford; Curate at Northfield. A Dominican priest.

J. T. D. Turnbull, of the Record Office.

Lady Caroline Townley.

Miss L. Taunton, daughter of Sir John Taunton.

Major F. Trevor.

F. W. Tarleton, barrister-at-law.

Rev. William Traies, M.A., Fellow of Merton College, Oxford; curate of St. John the Evangelist, Holborn.

J. Toovey, the Piccadilly publisher.

Dr. Twycross (Oxford).

Major C. Lennox Tredcroft, J.P., R.H.A.

Mrs. C. L. Tredcroft, daughter of the late Sir William Scott, of Ancrum, Bart., M.P.

Mrs. Tayler, widow of Rector of St. Matthias', Stoke Newington.

Charles Tregenna, B.A., Worcester College, Oxford.

Captain Trendell, of the Ryde Militia.

F. Trench, Balliol College, Oxford.

Emilius Watson-Taylor, of Headington Manor.

The Honourable Mrs. William le Poer Trench.

Rev. Henry Thompson, Curate at Ashford.

Thomas Trickett, R.N.

Mrs. Thomas, wife of late Rev. D. Thomas.

Captain Thomas

R. G. Tickell.

Mr. and Mrs. John Tharpe.

Mrs. Tracy Turnerelli, sister of Thomson Hankey, M.P., and cousin of Earl Bathurst.

Mrs. Trevor, daughter of General Trevor, of Plymouth, and wife of Brigadier-General William Cosmo Trevor, C.B.

Claude and Hubert Trevor, sons of the above.

Miss Temple, an East Grinstead sister.

Hugh Taylor. A priest.

S. W. Tucker, solicitor.

Mr. and Mrs. William Scott Tucker.

Lynall Thomas.

Mrs. Lynall Thomas, daughter of Captain Marryat, R.N., the novelist.

The Misses M. and F. Thomas. Nuns.

T. S. Tordiffe, of Bath.

Miss Townsend, daughter of a clergyman.

Mrs. Twycross, Gorton Lodge, Clapham Common.

Mrs. Harrington Trevelyan.

Mr. Twynam, solicitor, Rugeley; and Mrs. Twynam.

F. Till, solicitor, Folkestone; his wife and son.

Henry Tuck, Ingatestone Hall, Essex.

G. H. Thurston, surgeon.

J. Kellyer Tozer, of Cliffden, Teignmouth, Devon.

Mrs. Todd, daughter of Rev. Robert Hoare, B.A., and widow of Edwin Todd, Member of Colonial Parliament.

Mrs. Topham, wife of J. Topham, M.D.

Charles Trotter, of Woodhill, J.P. and D.L. for Perthshire.

The late Mrs. Charles Trotter.

Charles F. Graham Trotter, J.P., late of 93rd Sutherland Highlanders.

Miss Temple, daughter of Admiral Temple, Truro.

Marcus Talbot, Ennis, co. Clare.

Mrs. Tebay, wife of Dr. Tebay.

De Lacy Towle, solicitor.

U

The Hon. Mrs. David Urquhart, sister of Lord Carlingford.

Arthur Pollard-Urquhart, of Lincoln College, Oxford. A priest.

Francis Gregor Urquhart.

Mrs. F. G. Urquhart.

Mrs. Uniacke, widow of Captain Uniacke, Rifle Brigade.

V

E. T. Vaughan, B.A., Christ Church, Oxford.

Oliver Vassall, Balliol College, Oxford.

Rev. E. Vale, Curate of St. Andrew's, Wells-street.

Cecil Vernon and Miss Vernon.

Captain Vaughton.

Miss Vinning, the singer.

Mrs. Vansittart, wife of Rev. C. Vansittart.

Nicholas Vansittart.

Arthur Vansittart.

Bexley Vansittart.

Sir Francis Vincent, Bart.

The Hon. G. Vaughan.

Langton George Vere. A priest.

Miss Vinall. A Dominican nun.

Miss A. Vinall, Anglican Sister at Oxford.

Marie, wife of General Voyle.

Miss Vale, of Great Malvern.

Mrs. Ventris, wife of a clergyman, and the Misses Ventris.

The Baroness de Villefranche.

John Varley, St. Augustine's College, Canterbury.

W

Rev. Samuel Wayte, B.D., late President of Trinity College, Oxford.

Florence, Marchioness of Waterford.

Mrs. Walford, of Hatfield Place, near Chelmsford, daughter of Rev. Henry Hutton, D.D.

Rev. Edward Walford, M.A., scholar of Balliol Coll. Oxford.

John T. Walford, M.A., Fellow of King's College, Camb., and Assistant-Master at Eton. A Jesuit.

Frederick Walford.

Rev. Henry Walker, M.A., Oriel College, Oxford, Curate at Hardenhuish. A priest.

William Wilberforce, some time M.P., for Hull, eldest son of the Slave Emancipator.

Mrs. William Wilberforce, daughter of John Owen, founder of the Bible Society.

Rev. H. W. Wilberforce, M.A., Oriel College, Oxford, Vicar of East Farleigh.

Ven. Robert Isaac Wilberforce, Fellow of Oriel, Archdeacon of York.

William Wilberforce, junior, M.A., Oxford, grandson of the Slavery Abolitionist.

Arthur Bertrand Wilberforce. Dominican priest.

Francis R. Ward, Solicitor.

Rev. W. G. Ward, M.A., D. Ph., Fellow of Balliol College, Oxford, and late editor of the "Dublin Review;" Weston Manor, Isle of Wight.

Mrs. W. G. Ward.

Rev. J. B. White, B.A., Brasenose College, Oxford, Curate of St. John the Divine, Kennington.

Henry Waller, Barrister-at-Law.

Sir Bouchier Wrey, Bart.

Captain Granville Wood, R.N. A Jesuit.

F. F. Wells, M.A., Trinity College, Cambridge, son of Lady Elizabeth Wells.

Rev. John H. Wynne, B.C.L. and Fellow of All Souls' College, Oxford. A Jesuit-

Rev. J. Walker, M.A., Brasenose College, Oxford. Priest and canon.

Rev. J. G. Wenham, B.A., Magdalen College, Oxford. Priest and canon.

Rev. A. D. Wackerbath, M.A., Queen's College, Cambridge.

Rev. J. M. Watson, M.A., Caius College, Cambridge.

A. J. Walker, Emmanuel College, Cambridge.

Rev. Richard Ward, M.A., Oriel College, Oxford, Incumbent at Skipton. A priest and canon.

Robert Walker, Lincoln College, Oxford.

Rev. W. Wheeler, B.D., Fellow of Magdalen College, Oxford; Rector of New and Old Shoreham. A priest.

T. F. Wetherell, Brasenose College, Oxford.

Rev. W. Wingfield, M.A., Christ Church, Oxford.

Rev. J. H. Woodward, M.A., Oxford, Vicar of St. James's, Bristol.

Rev. Gresham Wells, M.A., Merton College, Oxford; son of Sir Mordaunt Wells; Curate of All Saints', Margaret-street. Now a Barrister.

W. W. Wardell, Architect.

Mrs. Wardell.

Charles C. Noel Welman, Norton Manor, Taunton.

Mrs. Noel Welman.

Rev. Thomas Wells, curate at Liverpool. A priest.

Rev. H. Wardroper, St. Mary Hall, Oxford.

Alexander Wood, M.A., Trinity Coll., Oxford.

Grenville Wood, barrister-at-law.

Rev. E. J. Watson, M.A., Christ's College Cambridge; Curate of St. Leonard's-on-Sea.

Rev. F. M. Wyndham, M.A., Merton College, Oxford; Curate of St. George's in-the-East. A priest.

Rev. William Winchester, M.A., Christ Church, Oxford. Chamberlain to the Pope.

Rev. J. Trevor White, Curate of Norton, St. Phillip.

Robert Washbourne, publisher.

C. Matthew Wayte, M.D., brother of late President of Trinity College, Oxford.

Rev. R. Webb, M.A., Lincoln College, Oxford; Vicar of Hambleton-with-Braunston.

Mrs. Wersley Worswick, daughter of Rev. R. Stephens, B.D., Vicar of Belgrave cum-Bristall.

Rev. Jabez Watson, M.A., Magdalen College, Camb.; Curate at Lostwithiel.

Charles Walker, Brighton; author of many ritualistic works.

General Webber.

Rev. J. P. Warmoll, Curate of St. Barnabas, Pimlico. Priest.

Mr. and Mrs. Fred Goulbourne Walpole.

C. W. Wyatt.

Rev. Wm. A. Weguelin, B.A. Cambridge; Vicar of South Stoke.

Major H. L. Wickham.

Rev. E. H. Woodall, M.A., Exeter College, Oxford; Rector of St. Margaret's, Canterbury. A priest.

Ch. D. R. Williamson, B.A., University College, Oxford, only son of Col. Williamson of Perth. Priest of the Oratory.

B. A. Westermann, Oriel College, Oxford.

William Whitmee. Priest.

Mrs. Wrey, sister-in-law of Sir Bouchier Wrey, Bart.

Mrs. Wait, daughter of J. C. M. Bellew, the elocutionist.

Rev. C. and Mrs. Whish.

Frederic Waddy, artist.

Mrs. Webber, wife of Sub-Dean of St. Paul's.

Mrs. Woodward, wife of Vicar of Folkestone.

Matthew Woodward, son of the Vicar.

Mrs. Ward, wife of Vicar of St. Raphael's, Bristol.

A. J. Wallace, M.A., Cambridge. A priest.

R. Williams, M.A., Oriel College, Oxford.

Walter Workman, B.A., Queen's College, Oxford.

Rev. Samuel Ware, curate of Bedford Leigh.

Arthur Wilson, M.A., Christ Church, Oxford.

Titus Hibbert Ware, of Halfbarns, Cheshire.

Rev. B. Wilson, Vicar of Fordham.

Rev. Edmund A. Willett, M.A., Cambridge, Vicar in the Diocese of Ely.

W. H. J. Weale, Archæologist.

Frederic Westlake, Professor at Royal Academy of Music.

Philip Westlake.

Nath. Westlake.

Mrs. Waring.

Frances, wife of Dr. Wootten, of Oxford, matron of Dr. Newman's school at Birmingham.

Miss Corry Wallace, daughter of Colonel Wallace.

William Wasteneys, Barrister-at-law.

Mrs. William Wasteneys.

The Lady Dorothy Walpole, daughter of Earl of Orford.

The Lady Maude Walpole, daughter of Earl of Orford.

Professor Wingham, Royal Academy of Music.

The Honourable Mrs. Woulfe, daughter of Lord Graves.

The Lady Webster.

The Misses Ward, daughters of the Hon. and Rev. Henry Ward, of Killinchy, Co. Down.

Rev. W. H. Wilson, M.A., Queen's College, Cambridge; Curate at Frome Selwood. A priest.

Miss Edith Whitfield.

Captain and Mrs. Wilde.

Miss Nona Warburton.

Mrs. Walter Workman.

Mrs. Wordsworth, the lady who survived the wreck of the Strathmore.

Mr. and Mrs. H. Wordsworth.

F. C. Collins Wilson, Trinity College, Cambridge.

William Wood. A Franciscan friar.

Hubert J. Wood. A priest.

The Misses Woodward, nieces of Lord Middleton.

E. Windeyer, King's College, London.

J. J. Watts, of Hawksdale Hall, Cumberland.

Eliza Harriet, sister of Sir John Eardley-Wilmot, Bart.

John Berry Walford, barrister-at-law, Trinity Hall, Cambridge.

Mrs. John Berry Walford, and a son and daughter.

Richard Walford.

George Wilson, quaker. A priest.

S. S. Wayte, father of the late President of Trinity College, Oxford.

Miss Wood, daughter of Canon Wood, of Canterbury.

Mr. and Mrs. Wellesley.

Miss Warner, daughter of a clergyman.

Mrs. Wood, wife of Canon Wood.

Mrs. Weguelin, wife of a clergyman.

Miss Wilson, Anglican Sister at Oxford. A Dominican nun.

The Misses Winthrop, daughters of Captain Hay Winthrop, R.N.

Ivan W. Watson, of Torquay.

Sir Charles Wolseley, grandfather of the present baronet.

Mrs. Walcott, wife of Colonel Walcott.

Miss Wildman, daughter of Colonel Wildman.

William Wagstaff, formerly of Forchabers, N.B.

Mrs. Wyse, widow of a naval officer.

Mrs. Ward, wife of Dr. Ward, M.P. for Galway.

Miss West, sister of J. R. West, of Alscot Park.

Mrs. Wilson and Charles E. P. Wilson, of Kelso, N.B.

The Baroness Wartzburg, sister of Lord Lyons.

Mrs. Weston, daughter of Sir John Lethebridge, Bart.

Mrs. Waylen, and the Misses Edith and Elizabeth Waylen.

Miss Wilcox, now Countess de la Torre Diaz.

Miss Wingham. A Protestant nun.

Mrs. Wilkinson, wife of a clergyman.

Dr. West.

The Hon. Admiral Wodehouse.

Mrs. Mundy Wood.

Rev. C. F. Wordsworth, Magdalen Hall, Oxford; Domestic Chaplain to Marchioness of Bath.

Mrs. C. F. Wordsworth.

J. T. Withers, solicitor, and Mrs. Withers.

J. S. Woodroffe, barrister-at-law, and his wife.

F. H. Woodroffe, Indian District Judge, and his wife.

Captain Wilson, Edinburgh.

Mrs. Wilmer, widow of Lieut. Colonel W. Wilmer, H.M. 8th Hussars.

Y

Mr. Deputy Young, Knight of S. Gregory.

Rev. George B. Yard, M.A., Trinity College, Cambridge. A priest.

Rev. W. V. Yarworth, Curate at Westbury.

Captain C. Yeoman.

Rev. C. B. Young, M.A., Exeter College, Oxford.

Rev. W. H. Youngman, Cambridge.

E. Youngman, St. John's College, Oxford.

Pym Yeatman, Emanuel College, Cambridge; Barrister-at-Law and historical writer.

Mrs. Pym Yeatman and family.

Major Yard.

Dr. Yonge, of Liskeard.

Mrs. Younger, of Haggerstone House.

Miss Lilian Younge and Miss Olive Younge, daughter of the late Major Younge, H.E.I.C.S.